WHAT THE <u>REAL</u> CRITICS HAVE TO SAY

Laugh? I thought I'd never start!

   – Sarah, aged 10, VIC

Amazing characterisations, enthralling plots, vivid use of language. You might want to give at least one of those a go

   – Nita, aged 9, NT

My sister thinks you are a brilliant writer. She also believes she is from a small planet near Alpha Centauri

   – Jodie, aged 2, NSW

Hilarious … fascinating … amazing. Just three words I wouldn't use to describe your book

   – Hilary, aged 11, QLD

You are a master of language. Unfortunately, not the English language

   – Bruno, aged 43, WA

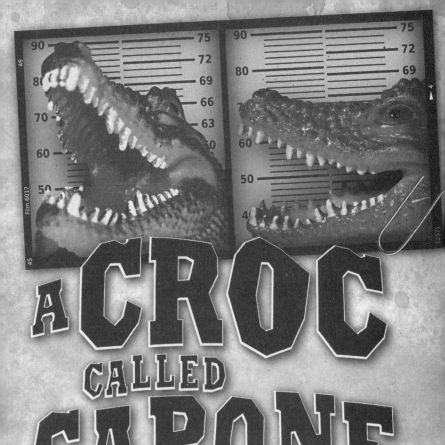

A CROC CALLED CAPONE

BARRY JONSBERG

ALLEN & UNWIN

First published in 2009

Allen & Unwin
83 Alexander Street
Crows Nest NSW 2065
Australia
 Phone (61 2) 8425 0100
   Fax (61 2) 9906 2218
 Email info@allenandunwin.com
   Web www.allenandunwin.com

National Library of Australia Cataloguing-in-Publication entry

 Jonsberg, Barry, 1951–
 A croc called Capone

 For primary school age.
 ISBN: 978 174175 668 5 (pbk.)

 A823.4

Printed in Australia by McPherson's Printing Group
Set in 10/14 pt Lino Letter by Bruno Herfst

10 9 8 7 6 5 4 3 2 1

www.allenandunwin.com

For Jasmin and Mya

Here's an interesting fact.

Crocodiles are, generally speaking, not fussy about dental hygiene.

I know this because I've stared into a large saltwater crocodile's gaping jaws. I stared because it's hard not to. Trust me on this.

Imagine. I was sitting on a muddy riverbank, soaking wet and filthy. My best friend Dylan was at my side. Next to him was a small, dirty-white dog. Not three metres from my face, a five-metre saltie eyed us as if choosing an entree from a dinner menu. It opened its jaws and slithered closer. Rows of sharp yellowed teeth loomed. Judging by the chunks of flesh-coloured material lodged firmly between its impressive incisors, this was a croc that wasn't overly bothered about a two-minute brush before bedtime. I'd be willing to bet it *never* flossed.

Dyl and I were in a bad position.

What made it worse was another six crocs circling to our left and right. True, they weren't as big as the monster in front of us, but you'd have to be amazingly optimistic to take any comfort from that. We were surrounded.

'Well, Dyl,' I sighed. 'At least things can't get any worse.'

And then they did.

The dog farted.

Even the croc blinked and moved back a pace. It might have fancied itself as the most efficient killing machine on the planet, but this fart was a weapon of mass destruction. I was almost hoping the croc would just attack and put us out of our misery.

How did we get into this situation? I thought. *Sitting on a slimy mound of mud, surrounded by man-eating crocs and enveloped in a fog of sulphurated hydrogen?*

I knew the answer to that.

It all started six weeks ago …

'A little pain never hurt anybody,' said Rose. 'You are such a sook, Mucus.'

At any other time, I might have questioned the truth of both these statements. As it was, I came up with the best reply I could manage under the circumstances.

'Oooooowwwww ...'

The thing is, when you have your head clamped under someone's arm and that someone is rubbing their knuckles – very, very hard – across the top of your scalp, it's difficult to find an intelligent response.

'If you mess up this holiday, Mucus,' continued Rose, 'I'll make you wish you'd never been born.'

I *did* wish I'd never been born. It felt as if my brain was being beaten with small baseball bats wrapped in barbed wire. The pain brought tears to my eyes.

'I won't. I swear I won't.'

I read somewhere about prisoners of war being tortured for information. Really nasty people stuck slices of bamboo underneath prisoners' fingernails. Or beat them on the

soles of the feet with red-hot paddles. Or gave them electric shocks on tender body parts. In the stories I read, the guys being tortured *always* kept their secrets. Lying there, on my bedroom floor, pinned under Rose's sweaty armpit, I knew I would not only give up all information in three seconds flat, I'd *make up* secrets, just so I could spill them.

Maybe I *am* a sook.

Anyway, I was prepared to say anything Rose wanted, if only she'd stop mashing my head to jelly. But as it turned out, it didn't matter what I said. She carried on hurting me regardless.

Rose likes dishing out pain. It's that simple.

'Swear you'll behave yourself!' she said, her knuckles grinding away somewhere just behind my eyes.

'I swear.'

'On what?'

Good question. What could I swear on?

'A stack of Bibles,' I gasped.

'You're not religious.' I could hear suspicion in her voice. And a touch of vicious glee that she'd spotted the flaw in my answer.

'I swear to God I am,' I said.

I have no idea why, but this seemed to satisfy her. It might have something to do with Rose having the brains of a flea. She let go of my head and stormed out of my bedroom, slamming the door. I slumped the few remaining centimetres to the carpet. It smelt very slightly of dog poo.

I clutched my aching skull in both hands and wished I had never been born.

Allow me to introduce myself.

My name is not Mucus. That's just Rose's little joke. You see, mucus is slimy, gross stuff. It normally drips from your nose, but in Rose's case it comes straight from her brain. I am Marcus Hill. I am eleven years old and average in nearly everything. Maths, Science, English, Art. I am slightly below average in height, which makes me a less-than-average goalkeeper in my local under-thirteen soccer team.

Average.

It's not a good word.

As words go, it's pretty average.

But …

In one area I am not only *not* average, I am exceptional. You see, I have a super-power. Only one person in four million can do what I can do. It's nothing to do with X-ray vision or leaping off tall buildings in unnaturally tight-fitting costumes to beat up improbable villains.

I'm not going to tell you what it is just yet. There are two reasons for this. First, I want to build suspense within the story. Second, I like being annoying.

So I'll tell you about my sister Rose instead. You have already met her and probably formed your own opinions. I'll just fill in some of the blanks.

Rose is fifteen and isn't average in anything, as far as Mum and Dad are concerned. If Rose sprouted wings and a halo popped up over her head, they wouldn't be surprised in the slightest. She aces all her subjects in school, which is no mean trick when you have the brains of a flea. She is a talented actress. Her artwork has been exhibited in a local gallery. There's a strong possibility her poo smells of violets, but I am not prepared to check this out.

Where I am average, Rose is perfect.

Except …

You know those stories about vampires? How seemingly ordinary people who hold down normal jobs and move among us unnoticed turn into blood-sucking monsters when the full moon peeps from behind a passing cloud?

That's Rose.

I don't mean she has pointy teeth and sleeps in a coffin, though nothing about her would surprise me. It's just that when no one else is around, she undergoes a dramatic change. Gone is the golden angel child. The wings crumble into dust, the halo turns rusty. Enter the spawn of Satan. Gleaming red eyes. Head that can spin three hundred and sixty degrees. Pure evil. In other circumstances, she'd probably go on a rampage around town, sinking fangs into the necks of innocent folk. But Rose is interested in only one victim.

Me.

This makes my life hard.

I've tied strings of garlic on my bedroom door. Didn't work. I keep a sharpened stake under my pillow. I'm saving up for a silver bullet.

As I said, Rose doesn't normally need an excuse to make my life a misery. This time, though, there was a specific reason. The holiday. The holiday Dad announced at the kitchen table during breakfast.

'Guess what, kids?' said Dad, peering at us over the edge of his newspaper.

I didn't answer. For one thing, my mouth was crammed with cereal. But the main reason I kept chewing was because we'd been through this before. Someone would say, 'What?' and Dad would come out with, 'The Dow Jones index has recovered from a slump in share investment after a bear market futures scare.' There is no answer to a pronouncement like this. You don't know whether to say, 'Bummer' or 'Excellent' or 'Pass the marmalade.' 'Please speak English' is an option, but I've never had the courage to try it.

'What, Daddy?' said Rose. She actually sounded interested. The sun streaming through the kitchen window reflected off her halo and made patterns on the ceiling. Her snow-white wings flexed. An invisible choir started singing.

'We are going on a family holiday at Christmas!' he said. He put his paper down flat on the table, the better to see our reaction. Mum stopped washing dishes and placed a

hand on Dad's shoulder. She smiled down at us. If this scene became any more Disney, I'd throw up my Weet-Bix.

'Oh, Daddy, that is soooo exciting,' said Rose. I swallowed hard. The cereal was keen to make a reappearance. 'Where? Where?'

'A wilderness lodge in the Northern Territory,' said Dad. 'Fourteen days. Accommodation, food, trips out – river cruises, safari guide, the works.'

'It's your dad's bonus from work,' Mum chipped in. You could see the pride oozing from her every pore. 'He made more money for the company this year than anyone else.'

I have very little idea what Dad does at work. I know he wears a suit. I also know he spends most of his time on the telephone or on his computer. Buying and selling, he says. But when I push him on this, he says he's buying and selling money. How do you do that? I mean, if I've got a dollar in my pocket, would you buy it for one dollar fifty? You'd have to be a moron. But it seems there are plenty of people out there who do just that. Maybe he only rings up the mentally ill.

'Daddy!' shrieked Rose. She jumped up and threw her arms around Dad. If her nose travelled any further up his bum she'd suffocate. Mind you, I have to admit I was pleased too. I'd never been to the Northern Territory, but we'd done a project on it at school the semester before last and it seemed like a cool place. They've got crocodiles there. With a bit of luck, Rose would get eaten by one.

'Oh noooo!'

I paused, another spoonful of Weet-Bix halfway to my mouth. Rose had clamped a hand over her mouth, the back of the other hand pressed against her forehead. I told you she was a keen actor, but this was cheesy even by her standards.

'What is it, sweetie?' said Mum, her voice dripping with concern. She and Dad had matching wrinkled brows. This is the way things are in my house. I could be ripped apart by a pack of dingoes during dinner and no one would notice. Rose chips a fingernail and the emergency services are called.

'Oh, Mummy. Oh, Daddy,' moaned Rose.

Oh, puhlease, I thought.

'What, sweetie-pie? What's the matter?'

'I'd forgotten, Mummy. In the excitement, I'd forgotten I promised to spend a week with Siobhan at Christmas. Oh, Mummy, Daddy. Can she come with us? Please? Can she? Pretty please? If she can, I don't want anything else for Christmas. I swear.'

I put my spoon down. There was no way I could carry on eating breakfast. My stomach can only put up with so much. Just as well, because things took a turn for the mushier, though you might find that hard to believe.

Dad looked at Mum. Mum looked at Dad. Rose looked at both of them. They all smiled. Small, cute, furry animals performed a song-and-dance routine across the table-cloth.

'I suppose so, sweetie,' said Dad eventually. 'After all, I'm not paying for the four of us, so I guess we can afford to bring your friend along as well. Sure. Let's go for it.'

Rose shrieked. She jumped up and down. She howled with joy. She hugged Mum and Dad. They hugged her back.

I watched. Beams of sunlight played around the kitchen. Pearly white teeth flashed. Cartoon chipmunks turned somersaults over the milk jug.

Time for Marcus to introduce a reality check.

'Okay,' I said. Three pairs of eyes turned to me. There was faint surprise in them, as if they'd forgotten I was there. 'If Rose can bring her friend, then I guess I'll be able to invite Dylan.'

The sun vanished behind a black cloud. Furry critters disappeared with a pop. A clap of thunder shook the room. Lightning crackled. Everyone except me aged twenty years. There was a silence so heavy you'd need a forklift truck to shift it. I tried lifting an eyebrow expressively.

''S only fair,' I added.

And it was.

If you can ever say that inviting Dylan to anything could possibly count as fair.

It's like this.

Dylan is my best friend.

Siobhan is Rose's best friend.

At least it's easy to pronounce Dylan's name. Apparently, Siobhan should be pronounced 'Shuh-varn'. So why didn't her parents just call her Shuhvarn, then? Were they deliberately trying to confuse people? I refuse to have a bar of it. I call her Cy Ob Han, which at least sounds like a minor character from Star Wars. And it really annoys Rose, which is a bonus. Rose, pronounced 'Loo-za'.

Anyway, Dylan. I could give you a rundown on Dyl. But it's easier if you follow me as I leave the stunned kitchen table, go to my bedroom, get into my uniform, have my skull jack-hammered by Rose, walk to school and enter the playground …

'Yo, Dyl,' I said.

Dyl sat on a wall, drinking a can of cola. Dyl is always drinking cola. He's so full of sugar that if he had a bath he'd dissolve.

'Hi, Marc,' he said.

'What are you doing for Christmas?'

Dylan frowned. He has trouble with the concept of time. He has no real idea what he is going to be doing in the next thirty seconds. Christmas was six weeks away. Might as well have been six years.

'No idea, mate,' he said.

'Well ...'

But I got no further.

A couple of kids passed by, handballing a footy to each other. Dylan jumped off the wall, intercepted a pass and kicked the ball onto the gym roof. It bounced a couple of times and then settled into the gutter. If Dyl had been anyone else, there might have been trouble. But no one wanted to fight Dylan. It's not that he's big and scary. He's smaller than me. But everyone knew that if you picked a fight with Dylan, he never gave up. He's as mad as a dunny rat.

'Dylan! That's my footy,' whined one of the kids.

'No worries,' said Dyl. 'I'll get it back.'

There are very strict rules at school. No one is allowed to climb onto buildings to get balls back. You must tell a teacher, who will inform the school janitor, who will, when he has a spare moment, take a ladder and clear the roof of all the stuff that finds its way there. This takes time. Normally, if you lose a footy up there, you're married with grandchildren by the time the janitor gets around to returning it.

But the rules are very clear.

Which is one reason why Dyl likes to blur them.

He shinned up the drainpipe like a greased ferret, hooked a leg over the gym wall, dangled for a second just for the sheer drama of it and then pulled himself onto the roof. Miss Lyons was on yard duty. It took her a moment to realise what was going on. When she followed the eyes of the kids in the playground, hers came out on stalks and a thin jet of coffee spurted from her nose.

'Dylan Smith! Get down this instant!'

Dylan didn't. He waved. He smiled. He strutted along the edge of the roof like a tightrope walker, hands out to the side.

'Dylan!' yelled Miss Lyons. 'Remember what we have said about this behaviour. You have a choice. You can escalate or you can defuse. Which is it?'

This was standard stuff. The school's policy on bad behaviour was to remind kids that they could either make things worse – escalate – or they could make things better – defuse. I have no idea what they hoped to achieve with this. It's no choice at all for someone like Dylan.

He escalated.

He stood on his hands and walked upside-down along the guttering.

Miss Lyons turned white.

The rest of us cheered.

Finally, Dylan flipped onto his feet, picked up the footy and hoofed it into the playground. Then he turned his back, dropped his dacks and mooned us. The cheering escalated as well.

I didn't see him again until lunch.

'Dyl,' I said. 'Remember I was asking what you were doing for Christmas?'

'No,' he said.

'Well …'

But I got no further.

Miss Prentice, the Principal of the school, loomed in front of us like a ghastly nightmare. She had a bucket in one hand, a mop in the other.

'Dylan,' she said. Her face was covered in lines. She looked really old. She'd not always looked that old. She'd actually looked quite youthful until Dylan enrolled. 'You were on internal suspension this morning.'

'Was I?' said Dylan.

'You spent the morning in my office. I allowed you to visit the toilet once. It seems someone stuffed a roll of toilet paper down one of the toilets and then flushed repeatedly until the entire boys' convenience block was flooded. I just have one question, Dylan. Why?'

Dylan frowned in concentration.

'Science experiment?' he tried.

'Why, Dylan?'

There was a long pause while the cogs whirred in his brain.

'Why not?' he said. He smiled as if pleased with his answer.

I didn't see him again until after school.

'Dyl?' I said. 'Remember …? Never mind. Would you like to spend Christmas with me and my family? On holiday up in the Northern Territory?'

'Cool,' said Dyl. 'When?'

I sighed.

'Christmas,' I said.

'Cool.'

'You don't think your parents would be a bit upset? I mean, you wouldn't be around for Christmas and that's a big family thing.'

'They might. When would we be going?'

I sighed.

Welcome to the strange and wonderful world of Dylan Smith.

Mum and Dad gave it their best shot, but I had them over a barrel.

They couldn't retract their offer to take Cy Ob Han on holiday. That would have sent Rose into hysterics. They couldn't, therefore, stop me taking someone. I could sue them in the International Court of Absolute and Obvious Unfairness to Siblings. So they tried to persuade me that another friend would be a better option.

I pointed out I didn't have any other friends.

They suggested I try hard to make one in the next six weeks. Failing that, we could take a complete stranger. An axe-wielding homicidal maniac, at a pinch. Anyone except Dylan.

Mum and Dad have banned Dyl from our home on the grounds that they like the house the way it is. Still standing. I was firm. No amount of bullying from parents would budge me. Dylan was coming.

Finally, Mum and Dad had to rely on their last, faint hope. That Dylan's parents had other plans. That they would cherish the moment when their son opened his presents on Christmas morning. That they couldn't bear to be separated from him.

It was a *very* long shot.

I gave Dad Dyl's home number and he rang and arranged for us to go round that evening to chat about the holiday. He drove Mum and me there with the desperate air of someone looking for a straw to clutch.

Dylan doesn't live in the best neighbourhood. It's the kind of place where even old people with walking frames dress in camouflage gear. We parked outside his house and Dad locked the car. He glanced back at it as we walked up the drive, as if not really expecting it to have wheels when we returned.

Dylan's mum and dad were really friendly. They offered us drinks, but Mum said no. I think she was keen to get this over with. Dad got down to business.

'Mr and Mrs Smith …'

'Joe and Mo.'

'I beg your pardon?'

'I'm Joe,' said Dylan's dad, 'and this is Mo.' Dylan's mum nodded her head and grinned. 'Joe and Mo.'

'Well, Joe and Mo,' continued Dad, 'we fully understand if what we are about to suggest is unacceptable, but we wondered if your son, Dylan, would like to come with us on a family holiday …'

'Yes,' said Joe and Mo together.

'The thing is,' Mum said, 'it's over Christmas …'

'Yes,' said Joe and Mo.

'Obviously, you'll want to know a bit about us and exactly

where we are going before you entrust us with your son's safety ...'

'Not necessary,' said Joe.

'Not a problem,' said Mo.

'It will be for quite a long time, right at Christmas ...'

'Terrific,' said Joe.

'Two full weeks,' Mum chipped in.

'No longer?' said Mo.

'You'll probably want time to think over your decision,' said Dad. You had to give him credit for trying.

'No,' said Joe and Mo together. They fell on their knees, sobbed and hugged Dad's legs. 'Thank you so much. Thank you. God bless you. This is the answer to our prayers, right above winning ten million on the lotto.' (Actually, they didn't do this last bit. But I think they might have if Dad had tried to back out.)

We left soon after. The car still had wheels, though a granny was eyeing it up and toying with a wheel spanner. We drove off into the evening haze. Or it could have been smoke from a burning building.

'They *are* strange people,' said Mum. 'Entrusting their son to complete strangers without even asking any questions. We might be murderers for all they know.'

'I suspect they're half-hoping we are,' Dad replied.

Dylan came round after dinner. I'd just made it to my bedroom when there was a rattle of stones against the window. This is Dyl's calling card, even though it would be easier to simply knock on the glass. I opened the window and he slid into the room. Mum and Dad would go nuts if they knew he was around, so I locked my door.

Dyl lay on my bed and opened a can of cola. He's a walking bar fridge.

'It's sorted, Dyl,' I said. 'You're coming with us.'

'Brilliant,' said Dylan, slurping at his can.

'We are going to have the best time, mate,' I said. 'Just you and me at Christmas. All that open space. Places to explore, things to see.'

'Fantastic,' said Dylan.

'You *are* pleased, aren't you?' I said. Sometimes it's difficult to tell with Dylan.

'You bet,' said Dylan.

'Any questions about it all?' I asked.

'Just one.'

'Yes?'

'Where are we going?'

End of term took forever to arrive, but eventually we made it to the last day of school.

It's an age-old custom that the final day of the school year is a muck-up day. So Miss Prentice suspended Dylan on Thursday. No one could imagine what would happen if Dyl was *encouraged* to muck up. The last day was fun, no doubt about it. But I couldn't help feeling it would have been more fun with Dylan there.

After school, I went to his place to help him pack. We were flying out on the Saturday afternoon and Dyl was excited. It was going to be his first time on a plane. I wondered if anyone had thought to warn the airline.

I mean, the last time I'd flown, the security had been really tight. You couldn't get a nail file onto the aircraft. I knew they'd scan Dylan, confiscate a nail file – though in Dyl's case it would more likely be a cluster bomb – and let him on. If the authorities knew him as well as I did, they'd wave through the cluster bomb and confiscate Dylan.

Joe and Mo wore broad smiles when they opened the

door. I got the feeling they hadn't stopped smiling since we offered to borrow Dylan, six weeks ago.

Dylan was in his bedroom, sorting through a pile of clothes that the Salvos wouldn't put anywhere near a rack in the op shop. He had a battered suitcase open on his bed. I noticed that most of the space in it was taken up with cans of cola. He glanced up as I entered.

'Whatyareckon, Marc? Two pairs of underdacks do me?'

'Dyl,' I said. 'We're going for two weeks, mate.'

'Yeah, you're right,' he said. 'One should be enough.'

I lent a hand with the packing. It took a while to persuade him, but eventually he got rid of the cola cans. I had to swear that cola existed in the Northern Territory. This left plenty of space and not very many clothes to fill it. The last thing he put into the case was a Christmas present – a small, not very well-wrapped package. I could see my name on it.

For some reason this made me sad.

I made a mental note to add a couple of pairs of decent boxer shorts to the presents I'd already got him. I'd stop off at a shop on my way home.

When I left, Dylan wasn't so much wired as plugged directly into the local electricity substation. He paced. He twitched. His eyes flicked constantly over his bedroom walls, as if judging the best angles to bounce off them.

I didn't envy Joe and Mo the next ten or so hours.

'Cy Ob Han,' I said. 'May the Force be with you.'

I nearly tripped over her as I walked up our drive. She had come round for tea. Again. For the last four weeks

19

Cy had been a regular at the dinner table. Apparently she and Rose needed every available second to plan for the holiday. What clothes to buy, what type of make-up to wear, which CDs to take along and a million other completely stupid things. I mean, what's there to think about? Stick some clothes in a bag and away you go. Better still, get your parents to stick some clothes in a bag for you.

This time, though, she was staying over as well. I deduced this from the small mountain of luggage she was wheeling. It crossed my mind – briefly – to offer help.

'Get stuffed, Mucus,' said Cy, thus putting paid to the already slim chance of me helping out. She wiped sweat from her brow and gave me the finger. She and Rose graduated from the same charm school. I reckon it's good that they're best friends. This way only two people are miserable, rather than four.

'Rude, you are,' I replied in my best Yoda voice. 'Swivel yourself you should.'

I opened the front door which, unfortunately and entirely accidentally, swung closed behind me. I could hear Cy cursing faintly on the other side. Naturally, I would have opened it for her, but I was in a hurry. I went straight through to the kitchen where Mum was preparing dinner.

'Mum?' I said. 'If Rose can have a friend round to stay tonight, why can't Dylan?'

'Dylan *can* have a friend to stay,' Mum replied. 'It's only you who can't.'

I opened my mouth and closed it again. Sometimes it's difficult to have a proper conversation with Mum.

When I made it back into the hall, Rose and Cy were

hugging as if they hadn't seen each other for forty years, instead of the forty minutes since school had finished. I don't understand girls. Their brains are wired wrong. Or it could be just a general design flaw. Rose glowered at me over Cy's shoulder.

'Mucus, you squirt. Get Siobhan's luggage in!'

'Love to help,' I replied with a cheery smile. 'But I've got a bone in my arm. Sorry.'

I was in an extremely good mood as I opened my bedroom door. Time for a bit of relaxation before tea. Listen to some music, maybe read a book.

I hadn't taken a step inside before the smell hit me like a fist on the bridge of my nose. The grin on my face froze. For a moment I was tempted to find Rose and ask her to knuckle my skull, just to take the edge off the pain. The paint on the walls blistered and peeled. I peered through the brown fog in my room. Visibility was down to a couple of metres, but I knew what I'd see.

A small, dirty-white dog sat on my bed. It raised its head from where it had been buried in its bum and gazed at me with pink-rimmed eyes.

'Wotcha, tosh,' said the dog.

You know how I said earlier that I have a super-power and that I was going to keep it a secret to build suspense?

Well, I've decided to cut you a break and fill you in right now.

About six months ago I was visited in the middle of the night by a scruffy dog taking a dump on my doona. This was the first of many surprises, very few of them pleasant. But the biggest shock, bigger even than waking up to find a smelly brown mound steaming under my nose, was when the dog talked to me. Okay, I know what you're thinking. Poor Marcus. Nutty as a fruitcake. That's all right, I thought that myself. But it turned out I wasn't loopy as a loon – no more than normal, anyway.

I have a gift.

According to Blacky – that's the dog's name – I am one of a rare breed of humans who can communicate directly with some special animals. It's like telepathy. I hear his voice in my head and I can talk back to him just by thinking the words. Doesn't make for a lot of privacy. If you believe

Blacky's statistics, there are only four other people in Australia who have similar powers.

Blacky is not a pleasant dog. He's not the sort of hound to sloppily lick your face and then roll over to get his belly rubbed. More likely to chew your nose off and then roll over to get a better angle for gnawing your ankles. Man's worst friend. And rude. Rose is sweetness and light in comparison. To make matters worse, Blacky also has a fart problem.

I don't mean he has a problem farting. He doesn't. That's the problem.

For all that, he taught me heaps. In particular, he taught me how we are destroying the planet and wiping out animals, plants and insects at a rate never before seen in the history of Earth. He made me understand how important it is to protect all living things, while we still have the chance. Blacky gave me a mission to make a small difference, a mission me and Dylan attempted together. It involved saving a ... hey, never mind. That's in the past.

When he left after we'd successfully completed the mission, I wasn't sure if I'd ever see him again. Given that he is grumpy, rude and smelly, you might think I wouldn't miss him. But I did.

So when I saw him sitting on my doona once more, I felt a rush of emotions. He sniffed his bum again. He's got guts, you've got to give him that.

I quickly closed my bedroom door. The smell needed to be kept in. If Mum and Dad caught a whiff, they'd either think a sewer line had burst under the house or I was collecting putrefying corpses in my wardrobe. My heart was racing and my lungs were bursting. I wanted to throw my arms around Blacky's neck and give him a hug. I didn't, though. He'd made it clear, early in our relationship, that if I was to ever throw my arms around him, they might not be attached to my shoulders when I was done. He is not of a touchy-feely nature. More growly-bitey. So I pinched my nose, walked across the room and opened the window instead. A bird flying past plummeted to the ground. I took a few deep breaths and turned.

'Blacky!' I said. 'It's great to see you.'

I even said it out loud. I'd got out of the habit of talking through my thoughts.

'I wish I could say the same,' he replied.

'Have you missed me?' I asked.

'Like kennel cough.'

'You've not changed.'

'Unfortunately, neither have you.'

It was time to take another breath, so I stuck my head out the window again. The bird was lying on its back, legs stuck straight into the air. It quivered, got to its feet and tottered a few paces before flying off unsteadily. I was relieved. Blacky told me it was my solemn duty to protect all living creatures. I didn't want to tell him he'd just poisoned one. And then it hit me, like a fart in the face.

'You've got another mission for me, haven't you, Blacky?'

'Naturally, mush,' he replied. 'You didn't think I came here just to see your ugly chops, did you?'

'Well. I thought maybe ...'

'Business, boyo. Business. And this time, it's a big one. It will take daring, courage, intelligence, determination and grit.

So, given what I know about you, you've got two chances. None and Buckley's.'

'But …'

'No "buts", boyo. Let's not go through all this again. You have a duty to help.'

'You don't understand.' I was waving my arms around, not just for emphasis but also to encourage the circulation of air. 'I want to help. I do. But I can't. I'm going on holiday tomorrow.'

'Holiday, is it?' Blacky sounded disgusted. 'Holiday? You know animals need your help and you'd sooner go on holiday? Typical human behaviour. The world is going to hell in a handbasket but, hey, let's lie on a beach and get skin cancer …'

'Blacky,' I said, 'I'm eleven years old. I don't have a choice in this. Won't it wait till I get back?'

There was a knock on the door. I turned as Dad stuck his head into my room. I whipped my eyes back to the doona. Blacky had gone.

'Marcus,' said Dad, 'your dinner's ready …' He wrinkled his nose. 'My God, Marcus, what's that smell? Either a sewer's burst or something's died in here.'

'Er … sorry, Dad. Bit of a bad stomach, actually.'

He pinched his nostrils closed and looked at me as if not believing anything human could have produced that smell. Then he grinned.

'Proud of you, son,' he said through gritted teeth. 'That beats me in my heyday and – trust me – that takes some doing.'

I couldn't eat dinner. I sat there, picking at my food. All around was the chatter of excited talk, but I couldn't pay it any attention. I blotted everything out and concentrated on trying to contact Blacky through my thoughts. Nothing. Eventually, I realised that Mum had spoken to me.

'What?' I blinked a couple of times. Everyone was staring at me.

'Are you okay, Marcus?' said Mum. 'Your brow is all furrowed and you keep staring off into the distance. You look like the bottom's fallen out of your world.'

'Judging by the smell in his bedroom,' said Dad, 'it's more like the world has fallen out of his bottom.'

'Phew. Yuck, Daddy,' said Rose.

I ignored them. I kept calling Blacky's name in my head. He didn't reply.

I had trouble sleeping that night. Under normal circumstances, you could put that down to pre-holiday excitement. Not this time.

I felt really guilty. I wanted to explain the situation to Blacky again, make him see that it wasn't my fault I had to go away. And he hadn't answered my question. Could the mission wait until I returned? Or was an animal going to die while I was having fun in the Northern Territory? Not that there was much prospect of fun. Not under these circumstances. I tossed and turned in bed. I'd left the window open in case Blacky came back.

He didn't show.

Finally, I got up. The alarm clock said five-fifteen and I knew there was no chance of getting any more sleep. So I slipped into shorts and T-shirt and cracked open my bedroom door. The house was quiet. I made my way silently to the kitchen, which was still shrouded in darkness, and fumbled towards the fridge. I needed a glass of milk.

I opened the fridge door and plucked the carton from the

shelf. When I closed the door and straightened up, I came face to face with a creature from your worst nightmare.

Time froze. A ghastly white face with red staring eyes loomed before me.

I screamed.

The creature screamed.

I think I had more reason. After all, I was dressed in shorts and T-shirt and my face was as normal as it ever gets. Average, you might say. This thing was hideous. Then I noticed it was wearing a disgusting nightdress covered with cartoon characters. The white face was vaguely familiar. It all clicked into place. I wasn't being attacked by a badly dressed zombie. It was Rose in some sort of facepack.

'What the hell are you doing, Mucus?' she yelled. 'Are you trying to give me a heart attack?'

How's that for unfairness? She skulks around in the dark, doing a terrific impersonation of the creature from the Black Lagoon, and I'm the one trying to scare *her*? There are demons in the deepest reaches of Hell that would soil their pants if they came face to face with Rose in a facepack.

'Why are you wearing that muck on your face?' I asked. Perfectly reasonable question, I thought.

She grabbed me around the neck and beat a quick tattoo on my head with her knuckles. It was only a short performance. She knew my screams were likely to wake the entire household.

'Beauty pack, Mucus? Getting ready for the holiday?'

Rose and a beauty pack. A bit like smearing five-day-old dog poo with moisturiser. You know it's not going to make

any difference. She needed something, sure. A garbage bag over the head was the solution that sprang to my mind.

We didn't get a chance to explore this idea because the kitchen light came on at that point. Rose quickly let go of my neck and ruffled my hair. She smiled, which made her look even more bizarre than usual because the meringue around her face cracked. She appeared to be impersonating a salt flat.

'Excited, Marcus?' she asked in a syrupy tone. 'Oh, hi, Mummy and Daddy!'

Mum and Dad grinned at us from the kitchen door. It was obvious that Rose's brief torture session hadn't woken them. They basked in this vision of sibling bliss.

'Couldn't sleep, huh, kids?' chuckled Dad. 'Neither could we. This is going to be a wonderful holiday. The great Australian outback. Nature in all its glory.' I could tell he was getting into the right state of mind. He hadn't worn his suit to bed, for one thing.

'It's going to be brilliant, Daddy,' purred Rose. 'I am sooo excited. What's the schedule today?'

'Last-minute packing, maybe brunch here,' said Dad. 'Then we're going to leave for the airport around eleven-thirty, pick up Dylan on the way. The flight goes at two, so I want plenty of time to check in. I'll rustle up some breakfast.'

Cy Ob Han turned up twenty minutes later, just as Dad was serving up the bacon and eggs. She had a facepack on as well. All we needed was a Big Top, a couple of lions and we could have run our own circus. After breakfast everyone went off to check their packing. For the hundredth time.

I went into the garden. The horizon was smeared with red and a couple of early birds were getting in rehearsals for the dawn chorus. Inside my head, I yelled as hard as I could.

'Blacky! Where are you?'

No reply. But it shut the birds up, which was a bit weird.

The taxi arrived at eleven-thirty on the dot. I slung my bag into the boot and watched while Rose and Cy loaded their luggage. There are rock bands on world tours that travel lighter. What were they going to do out there? Open a shop?

'Got your light sabre?' I asked Cy as we got into the taxi, but she ignored me. Luckily, it was one of those cabs that can fit in a hundred and twenty people, so she took the seat next to Rose, while I sat by myself at the back. It was only a short journey to Dylan's place. He burst through the front door almost before his parents opened it and would have shimmied through the taxi window if Dad hadn't opened the door in the nick of time.

Dyl plopped himself and his one small bag in the seat beside me. I desperately wanted to tell him about my visitor from last night, but that would have to wait until we were alone. So we peered out the back window as Joe and Mo waved us around the corner. I wouldn't swear to it, but I think they were carrying a bottle of champagne.

I wouldn't swear to this either, but as we headed for the freeway, I thought I heard fireworks exploding behind us. And possibly a marching band.

It's not often you hear a marching band exploding.

It took some time to get through the security scanner. Dylan was wearing his bar fridge jacket, and a can of cola in an inside pocket set off the alarm. He wasn't happy about handing it over to the guard and going through the scanner again. I think he didn't trust the man not to drink it. The alarm went off again. And again. Eventually, he had handed over six cans. I have no idea why he didn't just give them all up at the same time.

On the seventh attempt they found his Swiss Army knife.

'Whaddya mean, it's a security risk?' Dylan said.

The guard was built like a concrete dunny and had a sense of humour to match.

'It's a knife. You can't take a knife on a plane.'

'Why not?'

The guard just gave him a steely gaze.

'Well, when do I get it back?' said Dylan.

'You don't.'

'You mean you're stealing my knife?'

'No,' said the guard. 'I am confiscating it.'

'You can't do that.'

'I just have.'

'But it's mine.'

'You can have it back, but then you don't fly.'

There's no saying how long this fascinating conversation might have gone on, but I dragged Dylan away before things got worse. For the sake of the holiday I chose to defuse, rather than escalate. Plus, I could see the glint of hope in the eyes of the rest of our group. I knew what they were thinking. Maybe, just maybe, at the final moment, when all seemed lost, Dylan would get himself arrested and thereby save the holiday. I wasn't going to let that happen.

'That sucks,' said Dyl. 'My best knife! It had a thing in it that could take stones out of horses' hooves.'

'You reckon there's going to be a call for that on this holiday, then?'

'You never know,' he said.

'Excuse me, sir. You have been selected for a random explosives test. Would you please step this way?'

Of course they would pick out Dylan. Of course they would. We stood around yet again while Dyl was given a going-over with a security wand. At least this pleased him.

'Cool,' said Dylan. 'Just like in the movies. Do you want me to spread my legs and adopt the position?'

'You can adopt a whale as far as I'm concerned,' replied the security guard, showing there was at least one person in the airport with a sense of humour.

Surprisingly, no trace of explosives was found anywhere about Dyl's person. Mum and Dad looked vaguely depressed when he was given the all-clear and we trooped upstairs

to the departure lounge. There was still an hour and a half before our plane took off.

Dyl was overexcited. You could tell by the gleam in his eye and the way his muscles twitched, even when sitting down. An under-excited Dylan is too much for most people to handle. An overexcited Dylan is a disaster waiting to happen. So I took him off to one side of the room where there were a few arcade games consoles.

'Guess who came to see me last night, Dyl,' I said when we were far enough away.

'Paris Hilton?' he said.

'Whaaaat?'

'Well, I dunno. You asked me to guess. Do I get another go?'

'Never mind, Dyl. It was Blacky.'

'Whoah! You're kiddin'. Blacky the white dog? Does he have another mission for us, Marc? Does he?'

Dylan was my partner-in-crime last time Blacky had called. He'd had so much fun. More importantly, I think our success in completing the mission made him feel he wasn't useless, like everyone said. That he could succeed. That he had a talent. I know I couldn't have done it without him. Now I felt really sad that both of us might miss out on a new adventure.

Dylan's face was glowing brighter and brighter with excitement. I needed to dampen his enthusiasm before his head exploded.

'Yes,' I said. 'But I don't know if it'll still be around when we get back.'

I explained what had happened and how Blacky had left without giving any details. We mulled the situation over.

'Well,' said Dyl eventually. 'Nothing to be done now, mate. And at least you can be grateful for one thing.'

'Yeah?'

'You avoided Paris Hilton.'

Our flight was called and we joined the queue to board. Dyl and I had boarding passes giving us seats together. Cy Ob Han and the demented sibling were behind us. I let Dylan have the window seat because this was his first time in the air. We buckled ourselves in and settled down for the flight.

'This is so cool,' said Dylan after ten minutes or so. He was peering through the thick plastic of the window. 'The people look just like ants.'

'They *are* ants, Dyl,' I replied. 'We haven't taken off yet.'

I've said before that Dylan has no fear. The normal human instinct that makes the rest of us shy away from fire, for example, is simply missing in Dyl. He's more likely to stick his hand into a fire to see if he can use his fingers as candles. But, as we taxied along the runway, I noticed that his knuckles were white. I glanced at his face, which wore a matching colour.

'Not nervous, are you, Dyl?' I enquired.

'You kiddin'?' he replied in a shaky voice. 'Piece of cake, mate.'

But when the plane accelerated and we felt that force pushing us back into our seats, I heard him whimper. I filed this information away. Dylan was scared of flying. I had no idea what I'd do with this fact. It was enough just to know he was scared of something.

Mind you, it didn't stop him eating all of his in-flight dinner when we finally settled at our flying altitude. Even I couldn't eat the food and I'll eat just about anything. The flight attendant called it salmon tortellini with basil pesto. It looked like she'd thrown up in an aluminium container. Dylan ate mine as well.

Then we put on headphones for the movie, which was a particularly putrid romantic comedy. Dyl wouldn't normally watch bilge like that. Unless a movie had chainsaws, mutant monsters and fountains of blood gushing from severed arteries, he'd give it the flick. But now he watched as girl met boy, girl met other boy, girl had row with girl, girl learned the true nature of romance. Blah, blah, blah. Maybe he was hoping there'd be a dramatic plot switch. Girl gets sick of romance and sparks up a chainsaw. Maybe it was because the movie was free. Dylan liked free things. This probably explained his double helping of flight-attendant vomit.

Anyway, after half an hour I took off my headphones and left him to the wholesome fun. I closed my eyes. After the night I'd had, I could do with catching up on sleep. I nearly dozed off. It was only a commotion towards the front of the plane that snapped my eyelids open.

For a moment I couldn't work out what was going on. It seemed as if the entire first-class section was visiting the toilets at the back of the plane at the same time. I was puzzled. Didn't they have their own toilets? I thought one of the advantages of travelling first class was that you didn't have to use a seat polluted by an economy bum.

Then I noticed they all seemed distressed. Most were holding their noses and some appeared on the verge of throwing up. Possibly the movie was even worse than I imagined. Or maybe their first-class stomachs were rebelling against fish-smelling puke in an aluminium container.

I don't know which hit me first – the blinding realisation or the evil smell.

'Blacky!' I yelled.

'Wotcha, tosh,' came the voice in my head. 'That's cleared a bit of space. What's the point of travelling first class if you're crammed in like a sardine?'

'Can't someone open a window?'

The flight attendant was pale, but still standing. 'I'm sorry, sir,' she said to the man across the aisle from me. 'That's not a good idea at thirty-two thousand feet.'

'Can I have a parachute, then? I'm prepared to take my chances.'

I left them to their conversation and concentrated on the voices in my head.

'Blacky! What are you doing here?'

'Well, mush, at the moment I'm watching a particularly excellent movie. It's a girl-meets-boy-meets ...'

'Yeah, I know about the movie. *Why* are you here?'

'The mission, tosh, the mission. Even you can't have forgotten so soon.'

'But I thought that was back home.'

'Thinking isn't your strong suit, boyo. Best leave that to me.'

'I don't understand.'

'I've noticed.'

'Are you saying our mission is based in the Northern Territory?' I felt a sudden surge of excitement. 'That all the time you knew I was going on holiday there?'

'Amazing!' said Blacky. 'It can work out simple problems!'

'But *how* did you know I was holidaying in the NT?'

'Sorry, tosh. I never reveal my sources.'

'And how did you manage to get on board this plane?'

Blacky sighed in my head.

'I'm trying to watch the movie here, you twonk! Not field questions from a certified halfwit. However, in the desperate hope of shutting you up … I am, as I have told you before, a master of disguise. It is, therefore, but the work of a moment to avoid airport security measures. I always travel first class, by the way. If I was eligible, my frequent flyer points would be a wonder to behold. Now, I would take it as a personal favour if you would kindly shut your cakehole.'

'But what about the mission, Blacky? What does the mission involve?'

'I have my limits, mush. I have my limits. Okay. I'll tell you this much. Can you see a guy in an expensive suit? He'll be one of those who deserted the first-class cabin a few moments ago. Built like a medium-sized skyscraper? Head like a bowling ball?'

I craned my neck. People were still milling around the toilets at the back of the plane, waiting for the atmosphere to become breathable. I spotted him immediately. Blacky wasn't exaggerating. He was *huge*. Muscles piled upon muscles. And bald as a coot. Balder, probably. I have no idea what a coot is.

'Got him,' I said.

'Well, the mission is simple, tosh. You've got to stop him.'

After that, Blacky refused to say anything more.

I filled Dyl in on developments. He stood and peered back over the headrests to check out the muscled guy. Judging by the yelps from Rose and Cy, they obviously weren't expecting Dylan's face to suddenly loom up like a scary, loomy-up thing. It was small payback for the early-morning facepack terror, but I was grateful.

'Man,' said Dyl. 'He is *humungous*. What have we got to stop him doing?'

'No idea, mate. Blacky, the annoying little mongrel, refused to say.' I allowed this thought to roll around in my head, but the annoying little mongrel was still ignoring me.

'The size of him,' moaned Dyl. 'You couldn't stop him with a tank.'

'Yeah,' I said. 'Whatever it is, we are going to have to rely on brains and cunning.'

'You're on your own as far as brains are concerned,' replied Dyl. 'But I've got a black belt in cunning.'

It was true.

'Which makes us a brilliant combination,' I said. 'Holmes and Watson; Batman and Robin; Frodo and Samwise.'

'Kath and Kim,' said Dyl.

I sighed and closed my eyes.

We landed in Darwin. Briefly. The wilderness lodge we were booked in to was a further hour's flight, so we transferred to another plane. I kept my eyes peeled for Blacky, but

there was no sign. Not so the bald-headed mountain. He boarded the small aircraft ahead of us. I swear I could see the plane sink a metre or two as it took his weight.

'Why do we have to put our heads between our knees in the event of an emergency?' Dyl whispered to me as we watched our second safety demonstration of the day.

'To kiss our bums goodbye,' I replied.

Dyl just nodded.

An uneventful hour later, we landed at a small airstrip. While everyone waited for their luggage, Dyl and I stepped outside to have our first proper look at the Territory.

The first thing I noticed was the heat. It was like a thick wet blanket. A bead of sweat formed on the back of my neck, trickled and itched its way inside my T-shirt. The second thing I noticed was the sky. It was huge. Night was drawing in and the vast bowl above us was dusted with stars. Even as we watched, the sky darkened and pinpoints of light multiplied. I was amazed. I had never seen night fall so quickly, so dramatically. I saw the spiky silhouette of palm leaves against the sky. The sunset flooded the horizon with yellows, reds, purples. As I stared, the colours shifted, rearranged themselves. It was a miracle. The hairs on the back of my neck stood. I shivered with the wonder of it.

'Dylan,' I said, my eyes fixed on the glory above. 'Is that the most wonderful thing you've ever seen?'

'It certainly is,' whispered Dyl. Like me, his voice hushed with emotion. We stood in silence for a moment. 'Can you lend me a dollar?' he added.

'What?' I wrenched my eyes away from the sunset and

looked at Dyl. He stared at something away to my left. I followed the direction of his gaze. A cola-dispensing machine.

'Beautiful,' he whispered. 'Just beautiful.'

A guy waited by the baggage collection area. He held up white card which read BRANAGHAN WILDERNESS LODGE. A number of people were already standing by him, including our target, Goliath.

Mum and Dad lugged our cases off the conveyor belt and we moved to join the group. Rose and Cy Ob Han were wheeling their own personal mountains. We identified ourselves to the card-carrying dude, who checked our names off a list, looked at the luggage and scratched his chin.

'Congratulations,' he said. 'You are the proud owners of the tallest structure in the NT.'

Most sign-toting guys I'd seen at airports sported clean white shirts, ties and designer mobile phones. This man wore very short shorts. Judging by the stains on them, they hadn't visited a washing machine since 1989. His ripped singlet was decorated with patches of sweat. Scuffed plastic thongs. Compared to him, Dylan looked well dressed.

The scruffbag addressed the assembled throng. 'Welcome to the Territory, guys. And welcome to the Branaghan Wilderness Lodge Resort. I'm Ted, owner and manager. If you'll follow me, I've got the Resort minibus outside. It's a forty-minute drive through the bush. No worries.'

Dylan and I kept pace with him as he led us to the car-park. Ted eyed Dyl up and down.

'Good to see one of you is dressed properly,' he said.

'You're in the Territory, now. Comfort is the key.' He looked at my clothes and frowned. 'I hope you brought something lighter to wear.'

'Do most people dress like you, then?' I asked.

'Me?' said Ted. He glanced down at his ripped singlet, stained shorts and flapping thongs. 'No worries. I've made an effort, mate. Up here, this counts as formal wear.'

Forty minutes of driving, most of it down a dirt track, brought us to the Branaghan Wilderness Resort. I spent the time staring at the back of Goliath's head. He had taken the seat in front of me. It was fascinating. I'd never seen anyone who had a six-pack on his *neck*.

The resort looked great. I was relieved. Judging by Ted's appearance, there was a good chance the resort would be five battered caravans in a clearing with a dripping hosepipe in the centre. I had visions of him waving towards a rusting scrapyard and saying, 'Up here, this counts as five-star luxury. No worries.'

There was a huge swimming pool in the middle of the resort, glowing blue and casting slivers of reflected light. A large wooden building stood next to the pool and there was a good number of people sitting on the expanse of outside decking, eating. A proper restaurant, with dim lighting and black-dressed waiters.

Ted drove past the restaurant and stopped at a building signposted RECEPTION. Mum and Dad sorted out registration and collected keys. Then we walked up a path past rows of cabins until we found ours. Three in a row. I was relieved Dyl and I had our own. It hadn't occurred to me to ask before about sleeping arrangements. I couldn't imagine anyone would've thought it a good idea for me and Dyl to bunk down with Rose and Cy Ob Han. Particularly Rose and Cy Ob Han.

Dad gave one set of keys to Rose, another to me.

'Your mother and I will take this cabin,' he said. 'Rose and Siobhan – you're in the next one. Marcus and Dylan on the end. Look, twenty minutes to freshen up and then we'll head off to the restaurant, okay? I don't know about the rest of you, but I'm starving.'

Dylan snatched the keys from me and ran to our cabin. He opened the door, flicked on a light switch and stood on the threshold for a moment. I followed him up the driveway.

'What's it like, Dyl?' I said.

But he didn't have to answer. I joined him and we stood there in the doorway. Neither of us wanted to step inside.

The cabin was fantastic. There was a television in there and a fridge. Two beds. Table and chairs. Through another door we glimpsed a gleaming white bathroom. The furniture wasn't the problem. It was the smell.

'Oh, no,' I said. 'Not again!'

Blacky wriggled out from under a bed, shook himself and scratched behind an ear.

'Stop it, Blacky!' I said, wafting my hands in front of my face. You could *feel* his fart in the air, like a heavy curtain. 'Please stop it.'

'Sure, mush,' said the dog. 'Which way did it go?'

Dyl and I stepped inside the cabin and closed the door. I would have given almost anything to keep it open, but it

wasn't a good idea to have Blacky in plain view. I turned the overhead fan on full, while Dyl opened all the windows. Then I discovered the control to the air conditioning and cranked it up. The fog began to clear, but it was still like breathing soup.

'Well, thanks for the smelly welcome,' I gasped.

'No worries, mush,' said Blacky. 'Think of it as my version of a chocolate mint on the pillow.'

Dyl threw his bag into a corner and jumped onto a bed. 'Ask him about the mission, Marc. Ask him!'

'I see you haven't lost the brain-dead dropkick,' said Blacky.

'What did he say? What did he say?' Dylan was bouncing up and down in excitement.

'He said he's thrilled to see you,' I replied.

'Your nose is getting longer,' said Blacky.

'What's he saying?' said Dyl.

'Look,' I said. 'I can't hear myself think. Just keep quiet for a minute, Dyl, while I talk to Blacky. Then I'll give you a full report, okay?'

'Sure.'

I flopped down onto the other bed. Blacky curled up on the rug and gave his bum a quick sniff. He didn't seem disappointed with what he found. I tried to empty my mind. Past experience told me this was the best way to conduct a conversation with the foul-smelling mutt.

'It can't be difficult to empty *your* mind, mush,' came the voice in my head. 'It wasn't exactly crowded to start with.'

I ignored his insults. Experience had taught me.

'First things first,' I said. 'I still have no idea how you

knew we were coming here.' After all, I hadn't seen the dog for months and we didn't exchange postcards or keep in touch via Bebo. 'But tell me how you knew we'd be staying in this particular cabin. Dad didn't make the decision until about two minutes ago.'

'Call it a ninth sense,' said Blacky.

'Don't you mean a sixth sense?'

'Nope. We animals have four more senses than you.' Blacky flicked his eyes towards Dyl. 'And six more than him.'

'You're still the single rudest person I've ever met,' I said.

'That's exceptionally kind of you, tosh,' replied Blacky. 'Except I am not a person. Calling me a "person" strikes me as ironic, coming from someone who reckons *I'm* rude.'

I sighed.

'So what is it we have to do, Blacky?' I asked. 'I mean, I know you told me we have to stop that bald guy. But stop him from doing what?'

'Well, it's very simple, really.'

'Yes?'

'He's a murderer, boyo. And you've got to stop him killing again.'

My heart did a backflip against my rib cage. My tongue went dry and welded itself to the roof of my mouth. Just as well I didn't need it to communicate with Blacky.

'You have got to be kidding me,' I croaked mentally. 'A killer? That can't be true.'

'You're right, mush. I've misled you.'

I sighed with relief.

'I should have said he's a *serial* killer. That's much more accurate.'

As you can imagine, I had a whole new set of questions. But I didn't get the chance to ask them because, at that very moment, Dad knocked on the door to take us to dinner. Once again, Blacky disappeared in the blink of an eye. If he ever decided on a career change from full-time irritating gasbag, I reckon he'd make an excellent stage magician.

I was also getting very tired of Dad's habit of appearing at my door at exactly the wrong time.

The meal was memorable for three reasons:

1   The food was excellent.
2   Rose and Cy nearly clawed each other's eyes out.
3   I got to chat with a serial killer.

'Are you hungry, Dylan?' said my dad as we walked the fifty metres to the restaurant.

'I could eat a scabby horse between two bread vans, Mr Hill,' replied Dyl.

Dad blinked. 'Not sure that will be on the menu,' he said.

It wasn't. But other cool things were. I was really tempted

by the Croc Burger. I wanted to say to the waiter, 'Get me a crocodile and make it snappy.' But since I learned about the way humanity is destroying the planet, I've gone off meat somewhat.

Don't get me wrong. I'm not a vegetarian.

They eat vegetables and I've ruled that out of my life.

But I'm picky now. I want to know where the meat has come from. And I avoid anything with cruelty involved. I won't eat eggs that aren't free-range, for example. I'd probably eat the crocodile if I knew it was a volunteer. A croc tired of living. One that said, 'Dice me, slice me, stir-fry me. I don't care anymore.'

It seemed unlikely the waiter would give this guarantee, so I went for the barramundi special. Yes, I know about hooks and barbs and I don't buy the argument that says fish can't feel pain. But I was starving and you can only do so much. Anyway, who's to say vegies aren't in agony when they're ripped from the ground? What about a carrot's right to life?

While we waited for everyone to make up their minds, I whispered what Blacky had told me to Dyl. He drained his glass of cola and didn't seem in the least concerned. He glanced over to the far corner of the restaurant, where Goliath-in-an-expensive-suit had a table to himself.

'So what?' he said.

'So what? You reckon a serial killer is no big deal, then?'

'No,' said Dyl. 'I've murdered the odd bowl of Weet-Bix myself.'

I explained the difference between serial and cereal. He perked up then.

49

'Wow!' he said. 'This is going to be one cool mission, Marc.'

'Wrong, Dyl. This is going to be one non-existent mission.'

He seemed genuinely surprised. 'Why?'

'Look at him,' I replied. 'Two and a half metres tall, the same distance around his neck, probably one hundred and twenty kilos of solid muscle and hands that could snap you in two like a breadstick.'

Goliath snapped a breadstick at that exact moment. I winced. 'Exactly the kind of enemy I'd choose for two shorter-than-average eleven-year-old boys.'

'You're not scared, are you, Marc?'

'Yes. Terrified. I shake just looking at him.'

'I don't.'

'That's because, as you pointed out earlier, I'm the one with brains.'

We had to shut up then because the waiter arrived to take our orders. I didn't really pay attention to him. Call me silly, but a waiter is … a waiter. Stop me if I'm getting too technical here. He gave us his name – Brendan – and rattled off the specials, none of which involved horses, scabby or otherwise. Then he wrote down what we wanted and left. Ten out of ten for efficiency. Zero out of ten for interest.

But then I noticed Rose and Cy.

They were tugging at their tops and sweating. At first I put it down to the heat. It wasn't particularly hot here. Probably around thirty degrees, which was cooler than home this time of the year. But it *was* humid.

Rose excused herself and headed for the bathroom.

When she returned, I did a double-take. Instinctively, I checked to see if there was a full moon. Her lips were smeared with blood. *My* blood ran cold. I could see the scene in my head: Rose entering the Ladies, an unsuspecting woman bending over the washbasin, Rose sneaking up behind, a flash of sharp canines and a piercing scream as a fountain of blood gushed from a severed artery.

Then the penny dropped.

Lipstick.

And not just lipstick. She'd smeared her face with a heavy layer of make-up. Put a baboon's bum next to Rose's face and you'd have identical twins. Our table fell silent. Stunned, I guess. Cy Ob Han recovered first. She flashed my sister a decidedly unfriendly look. Then *she* headed off to the bathroom and returned looking like someone had applied primary colours to her face with a malfunctioning spraygun. Mum's jaw hit the table with a clunk. Dad choked on his water. Rose and Cy glared at each other and bristled.

I am not without skills of detection. I watch Crime Investigation programs on cable. Something was going on.

Another penny dropped. It was raining Pom currency.

The waiter.

He was about eighteen or nineteen. Now what makes a guy attractive to girls is a mystery to me, and I am happy for it to stay that way. But, judging by Brendan's appearance, having ears like windsocks and over-gelled hair in spikes is apparently no disadvantage. To me, he looked like a cross between Dumbo and an echidna, but to Rose and Cy he was clearly a chick magnet. I wouldn't have been surprised to see them leave their chairs, fly through the air and stick to him with a dull clunk.

When he returned with our food, the girls smiled and sat

51

up as if they had broom handles strapped to their spines. They were almost as scary as our giant serial killer.

'Thank you sooo much, Brendan,' trilled Rose, giving him the full force of her flashing teeth. Her grin threatened to split her face in two. He smiled back and Cy's face went in the opposite direction. She looked as though she was chewing cat poo.

'*Maaahvellous*, Brendan,' gushed Cy when he put a plate of something ghastly in front of her. It had yellow peppers and enough salad leaves to make a strong man gag. She had found her smile again and wasn't afraid to use it. 'Do you work here full-time, or is this just a temporary job? You know, while you backpack around Australia? And would you like to marry me and have four children?'

Okay. She didn't actually say that last sentence. But it's what she meant.

'No,' replied Brendan. 'I'm the owner's son. I wait tables, do a bit of maintenance, tour guiding, odd jobs.'

'How *interesting*,' burbled Rose who seemed annoyed she hadn't thought to ask the same questions as Cy. 'What tours do you guide?'

'Actually, there's one tomorrow. A crocodile cruise. Meet up at reception at ten, if you want to come along.'

'I'll be there,' said Rose and Cy in unison. When Brendan turned away to serve another table, they glared at each other. They bristled. I swear, if they bristled any more, they'd turn into paintbrushes. I almost expected Cy to whip out her light sabre. Rose would have been in trouble then.

Girls! If I've said it once, I've said it a thousand times. A waste of space.

All of this went straight over Dyl's head. He was busy getting himself on the outside of a large burger and fries and wouldn't have noticed if someone had set off fireworks in his shorts. But as soon as he'd finished eating, he pushed back his chair.

'Where you off to, Dyl?' I asked.

'Need a quick word with someone,' he replied. 'Back in ten.'

As soon as he said this, I knew. Sure enough, he headed straight for Goliath's table. I bolted down the rest of my food and followed him.

Look, I said I was terrified of this dude. And I was. But Dyl is my mate. What's a small matter of confronting a mammoth serial killer when it comes to looking out for your mate?

Well, a lot, actually. But I went anyway.

'Hey, Marc,' said Dylan. 'Meet Murray. Murray Small.'

Small?

I couldn't help myself. I automatically put my hand out and the colossus shook it. This was a worrying moment. Murray appeared very capable of leaving me with a bloodied and mashed stump where my fingers had been. Either that, or he would whip out a chainsaw and carve his initials in us. That's a popular choice among serial killers – at least, this is what my research of horror flicks suggests. But when he let go, my hand was still in one piece. I flexed my fingers and found, to my surprise, that they still worked. I sat.

'How ya going, mate?' said Murray. He had piercing blue eyes set among a nest of wrinkles. I could see the

reflection of the overhead fan sweeping over his shaved head. It was vaguely unnerving.

'Good. How are you?' I replied.

What was going on here? I had no idea of the correct way of conversing with a mass murderer, but I suspected 'How are you?' was not in the book of etiquette. But, when I thought about it, 'Do you prefer dismemberment or acid baths in the disposal of corpses?' was unlikely to hit the right note either.

'I'm really good. Isn't this a terrific place? I was just saying to your mate, here, that I come for a holiday at this resort every year. Can't keep away.'

'It's great so far,' I said. 'But it's our first time and we only arrived today.'

'I know. Saw you on the bus. But, trust me, you'll love it here.'

I hate to say this, but Murray appeared to be a very nice guy. He had a ready smile and he apparently wasn't bothered by two kids inviting themselves to his dinner table. Then again, killers must be able to put on a good front to the world. They live next door to *someone*. Hold down jobs. For all I know, they do volunteer work and video their kids at school performances.

'Can I ask you a personal question, Murray?' said Dyl.

Now. You never know with Dyl. It was fifty-fifty he'd come out with something like, 'Do you need good marks at school to be a serial killer?' So I held my breath.

'Go for ya life, mate,' said Murray.

'What do you do for a job?' asked Dyl.

Murray took a long drink from his glass, ran a hand over

his scalp and pushed his plate away.

'Guess,' he said.

'Wrestler?' tried Dyl. 'Bouncer, maybe. Hang on, I know. Bodyguard to the stars. You're an enforcer.'

Murray laughed. In fact, he laughed so hard he doubled over, his forehead almost touching the table. After a few moments he straightened and wiped tears from his eyes.

'Well, mate,' he said. 'I can't blame you. I sure look the part. Enforcer, hey? I wish. No, mate. 'Fraid it's nothing as glamorous as that. I'm a Consultant Paediatrician.'

Dylan's eyes widened. 'A what?'

'A doctor for children,' I explained. Dylan appeared to be relieved.

'So what do you do in your spare time?' he continued.

I think this was Dyl's attempt at low cunning. He was probably hoping Murray would say something like, 'Oh, this and that. Bit of serial killing on weekends and public holidays.' He didn't.

'Bushwalking, mate. Whenever I get the chance, I'm off into remote areas, mainly here in Australia, but also in other places. Africa, for example. It's my passion.' He glanced at his watch. 'Look, guys, I don't want to be rude or anything, but I'm really tired and I've got a full day tomorrow.' He stood. 'Sleep well, okay?'

'Are you going on the croc cruise?' I asked.

'Nah. I don't do cruises. I'll be taking myself off into the bush. A good long walk.'

'Maybe we could join you one time?' Dyl said.

Murray smiled and ruffled Dyl's hair. It didn't make any difference. Dyl's hair was already ruffled. You couldn't

squeeze in even a small additional ruffle.

'Sorry, guys,' he said. 'I go alone. No offence, but I see enough children at work.'

He took off down the path towards the cabins.

'He is just about the nicest serial killer I have ever met,' said Dyl.

'You meet plenty then, do you, Dyl?'

'Well, you know my neighbourhood.'

I glanced over at our table. Brendan was clearing dishes while Rose and Cy simpered, gushed and generally got in his face at every opportunity. I was starting to feel sorry for the guy. It was difficult to tell who was being more nauseating, but I think Rose had the slight edge. Then again, she'd put in years of practice.

'Can I ask why you decided to talk to our murderer, Dyl?' I said. 'Isn't this going to alert him?'

Dylan leaned towards me.

'Keep your friends close, but keep your enemies closer,' he whispered.

I was impressed.

'It's a line from a movie,' he continued. 'I've waited years to say it. I just wish I knew what it meant.'

We walked back to our cabins with Mum and Dad. Rose and Cy stayed at the restaurant to glare at each other and throw themselves under the waiter's feet.

'Don't stay up too late, boys,' said Dad. 'It's been a long day and I reckon we should be fresh for the crocodile cruise in the morning. Imagine. Seeing crocs in the wild! I can't wait.'

'Me neither. Night, Dad. Night, Mum.'

'Night, Mr and Mrs Hill,' said Dyl.

I *was* tired, but it turned out the day hadn't quite finished with us. We made it two metres up the brick path to our cabin, when a *Pssst* sounded in my head. I stopped and looked around.

'Blacky?'

'Follow me, tosh. I need a word in your shell-like.'

He sat under a low bush about thirty metres away. I grabbed Dylan's arm and pointed. As soon as we walked towards him, Blacky took off. We followed for about three minutes. It was dark once we left the small cabin lamps behind. I could barely make out his form as he climbed a bank to one side of the rough path. Dyl and I scrambled up behind him and stepped out from darkness into a world of pale moonlight. A white beach glistened, stretching as far as my eyes could see. Slow waves rolled in. The moon dappled the sea.

'Wow,' I said.

'Looks like paradise, doesn't it?' said Blacky.

'It does,' I said. 'It sure does.'

'Enjoy it while you can. In thirty years this will all be gone. This and most of the surrounding area. Global warming, tosh. Rising ocean levels will wash all this away. Hey. Let's hear it. Three cheers for humanity.'

'Thanks, Blacky,' I said. 'You really know how to ruin a scene.'

'It's called "reality", mush. And I'll have no lectures about ruining scenes from a human, thanks very much.'

We sat on a sand dune and watched clouds scud across the face of the moon.

'Global warming,' I said. 'Waste emissions thrown into the atmosphere that cause the temperature of the Earth to rise, because heat cannot escape properly. A bit like a greenhouse. Am I right?'

'Spot on,' said Blacky.

'Well, I know one way to drastically reduce the cause of global warming.'

'Ban fossil fuels? Find alternative and renewable sources of energy? Halt the worldwide destruction of rainforests?'

'That would work,' I said. 'But I was thinking of sticking a cork up your bum, thus reducing atmospheric pollution by at least a third.'

Blacky fixed me with one pink-rimmed eye.

'Very funny, tosh,' he said. 'Very dry. If you carry on being dry I'll have to pee on you.'

'Look,' I said. 'I'm sure you didn't bring us here simply to throw insults and then depress the living daylights out of me.' Actually, I wasn't sure. That's exactly the kind of thing Blacky *would* do. 'We need more information about this mission. In particular, Murray the Mass Murderer, who, incidentally, is a Consultant Paediatrician and seems like a very reasonable guy.'

'The important word there, mush, is "seems". Remember, there's no art to find the mind's construction in the face.'

It was the second time that evening I was impressed with a clever statement. First Dyl, now Blacky.

'Did you make that up, Blacky?' I asked.

'No. That was another genius. Shakespeare. One of the better humans, in my humble opinion.'

Humble?

'Anyway, I'm not going to *tell* you about our serial killer,' continued Blacky. 'I'm going to *show* you. Meet me here in the morning and you will see for yourself what this "reasonable guy" does on his bushwalks.'

'We can't.'

'Why?'

I explained about the crocodile cruise. Blacky snorted in my head.

'Oh, puhlease. You're not here to have fun, boyo.'

'Actually, we are.'

Now he sighed. The inside of my head was like a wind tunnel.

'Okay. But as soon as you get back from your fun-packed jaunt, you'll come with me. It's time for you to be educated, tosh.'

Later, I lay in bed listening to Dyl breathing. I'd filled him in on Blacky's plans for us, but he'd fallen asleep halfway through my explanation. That was okay. I was tired, too. In fact, I was just dropping off when I heard raised voices from the cabin next door.

It seems Rose and Cy were discussing each other's failings. Loudly. I couldn't quite make out full sentences, but female dogs appeared to be the major topic of conversation. I smiled. *A good day for dramas*, I thought, as I slipped under a final wave of tiredness.

But I had no idea – no idea at all – of the dramas that would unfold the next day.

The river was broad, sluggish and brown. The tour boat moved slowly towards its centre.

'Good morning everyone,' said Brendan over the PA system. 'And welcome to the Branaghan Wilderness Lodge Crocodile Tour. My name is Brendan and my partner Julie – give a wave, Julie – will be assisting me today. Before we get started there are a few emergency procedures I should go through. But rest assured, this tour has been operating for twenty years and we haven't lost anyone yet.'

Most of the tourists on the boat gave a small titter of nervous laughter. Rose and Cy laughed as if Brendan was the star turn at an International Comedy Festival. Then they glowered at each other, as he told us what to do in the event of the boat sinking and where to find flotation devices.

'I should point out, though,' he added, 'that the lifejackets are bright orange. Research has shown that crocodiles are attracted to the colour orange. So it might be a better idea to throw the lifejackets one way and swim like hell in the opposite direction.'

The laughter this time was decidedly more nervous, though Rose and Cy appeared to be on the verge of wetting themselves.

'One thing I can guarantee. We *will* see some crocodiles today. This river has the largest concentration of saltwater crocodiles in the world. You might not see them right now, but they are all around. Most people who get eaten by crocs have no idea what's happening until it's too late. As you may have noticed, the water is brown and murky. Go fishing on the side of this river, make a few splashes in the water, throw in fish guts and there's a good chance a saltie will be in your face – probably eating it – and you won't have seen him coming.'

Even Dylan was still paying attention and he normally switches off ten seconds after anyone starts to talk. Rose and Cy were all ears. A bit like Brendan himself. They were hypnotised. It reminded me of those old films about snake charmers – turbaned guys who play flutes and the snake's head follows the movement of the instrument.

The gel-turbaned Brendan gave us a rundown of the history of the estuarine crocodile, also known as the saltwater crocodile – not to be confused with the freshwater crocodile, which is smaller and doesn't attack people. It seems the saltie had lived pretty much unchanged since the age of dinosaurs. The reason for this is that the saltie is a superb killing machine and has no need to adapt. Its only predator is humankind.

I could almost hear Blacky snorting in my head.

According to Brendan, the saltwater crocodile population in the Northern Territory was now very healthy, though he

also said that until killing crocs was banned in the 1970s, numbers had sunk to a dangerous level.

'There's a proposal being considered by the government that hunting for crocs be reintroduced. But only by big-game hunters who are prepared to pay a lot of money for the privilege. This idea has provoked much argument up here. Some say it would inject money into remote communities and would have no impact on croc numbers. Others argue it is a barbaric practice, that we should leave the crocs alone. At present, it's illegal to kill a crocodile. Unfortunately, we do get the occasional trophy hunter who is prepared to risk the severe penalties for shooting crocs – up to $55 000 in fines and a possible six-year jail term.'

Brendan was being so interesting I was almost prepared to forgive his hairstyle.

Then he paused. All the time he had been talking, his eyes had roamed the expanse of water. Now he fixed on one stretch of the river.

'Just checking, folks, because it's easy to confuse a floating log with a croc. But if you look out to your left-hand side you will see we have company.'

There was a mad scramble to get a good view. Brendan killed the engines and we all piled towards the boat's railings. It was difficult to see at first. Then I spotted a V shape in the water heading straight towards us, the tip of a snout just breaking the surface. My nerves tingled. Julie – a blonde girl around Brendan's age and dressed in those cack-coloured shorts and shirts you associate with rangers or celebrity crocodile hunters – bustled around, fishing something from an esky at the side of the boat.

'Guys,' said Brendan's voice on the PA. 'Here comes Al. This stretch of the river is dominated by a very large male crocodile called Capone, or Al for short. And when I say he's large, I mean *large*. This guy is well over five metres. You don't get to be that size without being a ruthless hunter and also a fierce protector of your territory. No one messes with Al. Hence his name, like Al Capone of 1930s gangster fame.'

It was difficult to get a clear view. People were elbowing each other out of the way to get a line of sight. Rose and Cy were elbowing each other with *considerable* enthusiasm. Dad pulled me in front of him.

'You might have noticed that Julie is putting a chicken on the end of a rope, attached to a pole,' Brendan said. 'When Al comes alongside, Julie will dangle the chook and, hopefully, Al will jump to get it. Saltwater crocs jump when necessary in the wild to get prey, so we're not doing anything "unnatural".'

I could hear the speech marks in his voice. He was probably doing that annoying finger-twirl in the air but luckily I was spared witnessing it. All my attention was fixed on Al's approach.

'Most importantly,' Brendan continued, 'it's a great opportunity to get a photograph. So have those cameras locked and loaded.'

Julie brought the pole over the side and splashed the chook into the water a couple of times. Al glided closer. I could see knotty lumps along a portion of his spine.

But nothing could have prepared me for his sheer size when he glided alongside the boat. His head was huge and

63

the tip of his tail broke the surface way off to my right. This beast could swallow me in one gulp and I wouldn't touch the sides of his throat. Judging by the silence all around, the rest of our party was similarly awed. Al's eyes were flat and expressionless but his entire body radiated purpose. To eat. And you knew nothing would get in the way of that.

I wrenched my eyes away for a moment. I needed Dyl next to me, to share this with him. The crowd was tight and I couldn't see past the solid wall of bodies. I glanced to my right, towards the rear of the boat. Some small movement caught my attention. I was the only one who noticed. Everyone else's eyes were pinned on Al.

Maybe Dylan had tried to force his way through the throng and failed. Maybe he'd simply gone to the one place where he could get a decent view. Trouble was, in order to do that, he'd pulled himself up onto the railings. He balanced on a thin wire, one hand holding a guideline, his body arced out over the brown water, directly above the tail of the crocodile. I saw his feet tremble on the wire.

I've read that dramatic things often seem to happen in slow motion. To be honest, I'd never believed it until that moment. I saw Dylan's left foot slip on the railing. I saw the look on his face as gravity pulled and he tried to compensate. I saw his other foot go. But everything took an age. I wanted to scream. My brain gave out instructions, but that was in slow motion as well. The sound bubbled deep down in my diaphragm. The distance to my throat seemed impossibly far. I tried to pull away from Dad towards where Dylan was toppling sideways. My muscles, like

my vocal cords, were on a go-slow. I hadn't moved more than a centimetre or two before Dylan reached the point of no return.

He didn't shout, he didn't scream.

He plunged into the dirty-brown water, hitting the tip of Al's tail. Even the water arced up in a slow fountain as he went beneath its surface. The only part of the scene that wasn't trapped in a strange time warp was the crocodile.

Al Capone whipped round, the chicken forgotten. As Dylan's head broke the surface, the croc's slid beneath it.

And finally, finally, my scream made it through to my throat.

Imagine you are watching a movie on single-frame-advance and then someone presses play. That is the best way I can describe what happened next.

For the briefest fraction of a second there was stillness, a gathering of energy before explosive release. Then my scream shattered it, was joined by other screams, and there was a rush of movement down to where Dylan's head bobbed in the swell. Everything now was frantic, arms waving, voices shouting, rush, bustle, panic. But it was obvious to me – to everyone, I guess – that nothing we did really mattered. There was Dylan's head. There was a crocodile somewhere beneath the surface. Those of us safely on the boat had no power to alter events out there.

Brendan moved quickly. So did Julie. She picked up the remains of the chook and hurled it off to the left. Then she slung the bloodstained dregs in the bucket over the side. Part of me dimly understood why. She was trying to distract the croc, get the smell of blood to draw him away from Dyl.

Julie thumped the surface of the water repeatedly with the pole. Nothing happened. The river's surface was broken only by her pole and the splash of Dylan's arms as he trod water. We watched, horrified, expecting any moment to see Dylan yanked from sight, his arms disappearing beneath the water, the swell fading and smoothing until all that was left was the stillness of nothing. I tried to keep his head above water by sheer force of will.

Brendan threw a lifebelt over the side and Dylan grabbed hold of it. Other adults pulled on it, dragging him to the side of the boat while Brendan slipped over the railings and stretched towards him.

'Grab my hand,' he yelled.

Even leaning out dangerously far, Brendan couldn't reach Dyl's outstretched fingers. They clawed at each other, missing by a matter of centimetres.

'Pull on that lifebelt harder,' yelled Brendan over his shoulder. I saw Dad and the others straining on the rope. More joined them. I would have gone myself, but I was paralysed again. I could only stand by the railing and look into Dylan's eyes. They were strangely calm. And then, maybe two or three metres behind him, I saw the croc's head break the surface for a fraction of a second. Its eyes were calm, as well. Calm and totally lacking in mercy. They dipped beneath the surface once more.

My memories of that time are broken. They lie in pieces in my mind, so I am not sure what's real and what's imagined. But I think I saw this. I think I saw something beyond the line of sight joining Dylan's eyes and those of the crocodile – on the bank of the river, a small, dirty-white dog sitting motionless, gazing at us. Then I blinked and he was gone.

The people pulling on the lifebelt had established a rhythm now. They swayed forward and Dyl slipped back into the water. My heart hammered as I imagined powerful jaws clamped around his legs. But then the line leaned back and he surged above the surface. Brendan's hand grabbed his, slipped for a moment and then locked around his wrist. Other people wrapped their arms around Brendan's waist. They leaned back as he pulled. Dylan's body came right out of the water, his feet scrabbled on the side of the boat and then, with a rush, he fell onto the deck, tangled up with Brendan. They flopped around like fish.

I think I was the first to get to Dyl, but I might be wrong. I remember being on my knees as he struggled to get up. He looked me in the eyes. His face was pale and there were bits of rubbish in his hair – small twigs and slimy green stuff.

He grinned.

'How cool was that?' he croaked.

I didn't answer. Instead I threw up on the front of his T-shirt.

Rose and Cy were completely hysterical. They sobbed and wailed all the way back to our cabins. Dad was deathly quiet, but I got the feeling that, given half a chance, he'd join in. Even Brendan, who'd been the calmest while the emergency was going on, was trembling as he moored the boat and helped us disembark. Julie had to drive the minibus back to the resort.

Mum, on the other hand, went straight into protective mode. True, she was badly shaken. I could tell by the way her lips were set in a thin white line. She clasped Dyl to her so tightly on the minibus you'd have needed a crowbar to pry him loose. He winked at me from the folds of Mum's dress. I tried to wink back but I was numb and my muscles wouldn't work.

The resident doctor winkled Dyl out of Mum's arms and checked him over. According to the doc, Dyl was fine physically, but it was possible delayed shock would set in. He explained that it's not uncommon for people who have undergone a really nasty experience to be fine at first and then fold into trembling blubber later when the mind finally grasps what has happened. He ordered Dyl to rest.

Dyl wasn't keen on resting. It's something he's avoided all his life. But one glance at Mum's face convinced him it might be wiser to follow instructions. Or maybe he was worried she'd do her impersonation of a human vice again. I went with him to our cabin and Mum tucked him into bed. She ran a hand through his hair.

'You get some sleep,' she said.

'Yes, Mum,' said Dyl.

Mum didn't react to his slip of the tongue. Perhaps, like me, she put it down to delayed shock.

We closed the cabin door and joined the rest of the family at the resort bar. Dad ordered something strong for him and Mum and soft drinks for me, Rose and Cy. I don't think I'd ever seen Mum drink anything other than a very occasional glass of wine. Now, she took a glass of dark amber liquid and downed it in one. Dad got her another. The five of us sat around a table and for a while no one said anything. Then Dad broke the silence.

'I think we should see about getting a flight home.'

I nearly said something. I didn't want to go home. More to the point, I knew Dyl wouldn't want to go home. He'd be devastated. And, when I glanced at Rose and Cy, I could see the same reaction in their faces. But Mum jumped in before any of us could react.

'Of course we must go home,' she said. 'There's nothing else to do. That poor boy. And his poor parents. Oh, my God.' She bit at the corner of a fingernail. 'What will his parents say? We've only been here a few hours and we've nearly killed him. What kind of people are we?'

'Mum,' said Rose, 'it wasn't your fault. It wasn't anyone's fault. It was an accident.'

But Mum wasn't in the mood to hear that. 'Don't be stupid, Rose,' she yelled. If the circumstances had been different I would have been happy. It's not often Rose cops any kind of criticism. But clearly the sunbeams radiating from her bum were undergoing an eclipse.

'Your father and I are responsible for Dylan,' Mum said in softer tones. 'That is the deal we made with his parents when they agreed to let him come along. To look after him. To make sure no harm came to him. To ensure precisely that no accident happened. And we failed. There can be no excuses. And now we need to get him back to his parents. It's the very least we can do.'

'Your mother is right,' said Dad. 'I don't think we've any other option.'

I said nothing. There was no point. Anyway, I was worried someone would ask me what I'd seen out there on the boat. Everyone was making the assumption Dylan just slipped off the side. Only I knew that it was really his own fault. Who, in their right mind, would climb onto a railing and lean out over a man-eating crocodile? No one. But Dylan had never been in his right mind. If my parents knew him as well as I do, they'd realise this was completely normal behaviour.

I wasn't going to tell them that, of course. Dyl is barking mad, but he's my mate.

So I wandered off down to the beach, while Mum and Dad went to the front office to make arrangements. I'd have gone to the cabin – I was sure Dyl wouldn't be asleep – but I knew I'd be in serious strife if I was seen. Anyway, I needed quiet time.

Not that I got it. Blacky appeared at my side almost as soon as I reached the water's edge.

'Wotcha, bucko,' he said.

'Hey, Blacky,' I replied. 'Wassup?'

'From where I'm standing, just your head up your own butt.'

I wasn't in the mood, so I didn't say anything. I picked up a couple of flat stones and skimmed them across the ocean's surface. It was lovely here. I'd miss it.

Blacky sniffed around a patch of sand and then cocked his leg up against a washed-up branch. I watched the thin yellow stream dwindle and die.

'Well, boyo,' he said. 'You're back earlier than I expected, but that's all to the good. Ready for our trip?'

'No. What's the point?'

'The point, mush, is that you have a mission to fulfil.'

'Well, you can forget about the mission, *tosh*,' I replied. 'I know you know what happened to Dyl today. You can read my mind, after all. There's no chance of me and Dylan doing anything without being supervised by Mum, Dad and probably thirty hired bodyguards. And that would be true even if we weren't on the point of leaving anyway.'

'There are no flights out today, boyo. This isn't Sydney, in case you hadn't noticed. The earliest you'll be leaving is tomorrow night.'

'So?'

'So, tosh, you still have time to do some good. But time *is* running out now. Your dipstick mate has made sure of that.'

I skimmed another stone. It felt like I was carrying a heavy weight. This holiday was finished before it had properly begun. The truth was beginning to sink in.

I had no enthusiasm for anything.

'Look, Marcus,' said Blacky. His tone was unlike any I'd heard from him before. 'I know you're sad. But this mission is important. If you don't do something now, you'll regret it later on. When you get home. You have a chance to make a difference. Take it. While your mum and dad *aren't* around to spoil it.'

Did he call me Marcus?

I skimmed another stone and thought it through. Blacky had a point. Feeling down shouldn't stop me doing the right thing. Maybe – just maybe – I could salvage something from this disaster. Plus, I was curious about Murray Small.

What was it Blacky had said? That he'd *show* me what Murray got up to on those bushwalks. And I had nothing better to do.

'Okay, Blacky,' I said. 'You win.'

'I normally do, tosh. I normally do. Follow me.'

He took off down the beach. I chucked my remaining pebbles on the sand and followed. Despite everything, I felt my spirits lift. It wasn't every day Blacky was sympathetic to my feelings. It wasn't *any* day, come to think of it. He'd called me Marcus. He knew I was sad and felt sorry for me.

'Don't get used to it, mush,' came a voice in my head. 'I'll sink to any depths to get results.'

We didn't stay on the beach long. After a couple of hundred metres, Blacky climbed a dune and disappeared into stunted bush. I had difficulty keeping up. Judging by the foul smell I was wading through, he was using his bum as a super-turbo-charger.

'Blacky!' I yelled. 'Not so fast.'

'No time to waste, tosh,' he replied. He did slow down a bit, though.

The bush thickened and the ground underneath grew soggy. Once or twice, my feet sank into soft mud and I had to pull them free with sucking sounds. Pools of water were all around, as were strange trees with roots that bulged from their trunks and snaked down into wet earth.

'Mangroves, mush,' said Blacky. 'Fascinating things. Ancient. Pity your lot have bulldozed so many to build shopping malls, multi-storey carparks and high-rise apartment blocks. Still, progress, huh?'

I wasn't in the mood for another lecture about the environment. Anyway, a disturbing thought had struck.

I gazed around a threatening landscape. The air was thick with moisture and the whine of mosquitoes. I felt as though we were a million kilometres from another human being.

'Is it dangerous out here, Blacky?' I asked.

'Dangerous? No, tosh. Safe as houses.' He paused. 'Apart from … hey, never mind. Come on. Not much further now.'

I didn't budge.

'Apart from what?'

'Nothing, really. Just … you haven't got any open cuts on your legs or feet, have you?'

'I don't think so. Why?'

'Then don't worry about it.'

That was it. I wasn't going any further until he told me. Blacky sat on a small hummock amid the wetness and fixed me with his pink-rimmed eyes.

'Okay,' he said finally. 'It's just that there *is* a bug in the earth that can get into your bloodstream through small nicks in the skin. It only comes to the surface when it's wet.' I looked around at the flooded land. 'Little possibility of getting infected, though. You've more chance of being struck by lightning.'

I didn't point out that with my luck I'd probably experience both. I simply let a glowing image of a question mark float through my mind.

'It's called meliodosis,' Blacky continued. 'Can be a teensy-weensy bit nasty.'

'How nasty?'

'Well, not *bad*. After a while your arms and legs fall off. Then you die … If you're lucky.'

'Well, gosh, Blacky,' I said. 'Thank goodness it's only a teensy-weensy bit nasty. I thought I might be in trouble there for a moment.'

'Nah, mush. You're much more likely to be bitten by a snake.'

I was on the point of moving forward again. I stopped. 'Snake?'

'This *is* the Territory, tosh. Home of some of the most venomous snakes in the world. But I wouldn't worry, if I were you. After all, it's the crocs you've *really* got to watch out for.'

'Let me get this straight, Blacky,' I said. 'Apart from a bug that makes bits of you drop off and deadly snakes and man-eating crocodiles, this is a completely safe place?'

'Well, of course there's also ...'

'Never mind,' I said. 'I don't want to know. Lead on.'

Suddenly, I needed to get out of there.

This river wasn't as broad as the one we'd been on for the croc cruise. Blacky and I stood on the edge and looked at the body floating a few metres from shore.

'This is the doing of your mate Murray,' said Blacky. 'Your "reasonable guy". Tell me, bucko. Does this look reasonable to you?'

The crocodile's pale, almost white, underbelly bobbed gently. Its short arms floated to the side in pathetic openness. I don't know which emotion I felt first: sadness or anger.

'He shot it earlier,' Blacky continued. 'When you guys were on the cruise. Trouble is, he didn't kill it cleanly. It was sunning itself on the bank when it took a round in

the head from a high-powered rifle. Got into the water. Tried to swim away. Murray couldn't get to the body, so he just went off in search of other prey while this croc took half an hour to die.'

It took me a minute to find my voice.

'But it's illegal. He's a doctor!'

'Yes. And a big-game hunter. This is what he does for kicks, tosh. Not just here, but all over the world. Africa, South America. He's killed lions, elephants, all manner of animals. Endangered? Doesn't matter to him. If it's big and wild, he wants to kill it.'

I badly needed to sit down, but the ground was wet and we were very close to the bank. Suddenly I became aware of what might be lurking under the surface of that slow-moving river. I moved back a few paces.

'I don't get this, Blacky,' I said. 'Murray Small arrived yesterday. He couldn't have brought a rifle with him and it's a helluva way to the nearest gun shop. It doesn't make any sense.'

'He has money, boyo. Lots of money. It's not difficult to arrange for a couple of other guys to come here in a four-wheel drive with all the equipment he needs. Another thing you must understand. He isn't interested in skins or heads on the wall. His accomplices take whatever trophies they want from the slaughtered animals. He just likes the act of killing. And it means there's no evidence to connect him with the crime.'

I couldn't take my eyes from the crocodile's body.

'And here's a coincidence, mush. That's Al's brother floating out there.'

'Al?'

'Al Capone, the croc that nearly chomped your twonk of a mate. He is not going to be pleased.'

I ran my hands through my hair. There were so many things I couldn't get straight in my head. My hair was one of those things, but I didn't bother about that then.

'How do you *know* this stuff, Blacky?' I said. 'I mean, all that about him killing lions and elephants. You couldn't have seen that with your own eyes.' Then again, I thought, he'd managed to smuggle himself onto a plane to get here. I had a sudden image of Blacky in a gondola, sailing down a canal in Venice. Blacky in a pith helmet in an African jungle. Blacky taking a snapshot of the Taj Mahal.

'I gather information, tosh,' he replied. 'I am the hub of a national and international confederation of animals. There's not much that goes on in the world that I don't know about. Think of me as a masterspy. I send agents out into the field. I plan operations. I ...'

'Yes, okay, Blacky.' He was so full of hot air, it was a wonder he didn't float. 'I get the idea. And now what?'

'Now, tosh, you stop him. Before others die.'

I thought about Murray and people like him all over the world. Bringing death, not just to individual animals, but pushing whole species to the brink of extinction.

Blacky was right. It was wrong. It was evil. The killing had to stop.

But how?

'I can't do everything, boyo,' said Blacky. 'Try using that flabby thing you call a brain.'

I tried, but couldn't get past the fact I was a smaller-

79

than-average eleven year old and Murray Small had the
build of a larger-than-average rugby prop-forward. Plus
he had a gun. It was hopeless.

Impossible.

And that was when the idea hit me.

Blacky cocked his head.

'That might just work, mush. That might very well work.
Amazing. The human brain *does* function. Follow me.'

And he took off into the bush again.

It was twenty minutes before we heard the first gunshot,
another ten before we heard voices.

Blacky and I slowed down. We moved from tree to tree,
trying to sneak up on them. Not much of a problem for
a small dog, especially one who was also apparently a
master of disguise, but tricky for an eleven year old whose
feet kept getting stuck in foul-smelling sludge. The cover
wasn't great here, either, and the land was so flat there
was no chance of peering over a convenient hummock,
the way they do in movies. Luckily, the men were busy
dragging something up to a ute that was totally smeared
with red dirt and brown mud. They were concentrating so
hard that Blacky and I managed to sneak closer without
attracting attention.

It was Murray and a couple of other guys with long
beards. Rifles were propped against the ute's tray. One
man had a long hunting knife in his hand. I slipped behind
a tree and peered around the trunk. Even though I was
still some distance away, I could see what they had been
dragging.

It was the head and skin of a large crocodile. They must have gutted it where it had been shot. Now they spread the remains onto the ground by the ute.

Images flipped through my mind. Al's brother, his short legs splayed in death, bobbing on the river. Then Al himself, gliding alongside the tour boat. Powerful jaws. Cold eyes.

Terrifying.

Yet so beautiful.

I realised I'd stopped breathing. My hands were clenched so tightly that when I uncurled them, my nails had left crescent-shaped gouges in my palms. I exhaled slowly, calmed the anger surging through my blood.

I needed a cool head.

Blacky and I silently agreed on what must happen. Timing was crucial. We ran through it one more time. Then he slipped off across the wet land, crossed the thin trail on which the ute was parked and disappeared into the bush on the other side. I waited.

'Hey, Murray,' one of the guys called out. 'What about a photo of you with your kill?'

'Nah, mate,' said Murray. 'Not into souvenirs.'

'Oh, go on.'

'Mate, I said no. I'm not taking the chance of being identified should some photo fall into the wrong hands.'

The other guy laughed.

'You worry too much.'

'I worry enough,' snapped Murray. 'And if you don't like it you know what you can do. I can always take my money elsewhere. *Mate*.'

The man with the knife lifted his hands. A few drops of

blood fell from the stained blade.

'Whoa, man,' he said. 'No offence, okay?'

At that moment an unearthly noise floated through the bush. A howl that seemed to come from the bowels of the earth. If you were imaginative you'd think it was some spirit moaning in inexpressible agony.

Luckily I'm not imaginative. Anyway, I knew that it was Blacky.

The men were startled. They grabbed their guns and moved to the other side of the ute, out of my line of sight. This was the time to make *my* move. I slipped out from behind the tree trunk and sprinted towards the ute. Sprinted is a slight exaggeration. Given the muddy earth, 'oozed' might be a better word. But I made it to another tree approximately twenty metres from the men.

This tree had a dense canopy of broad leaves. Equally importantly, it was easy to climb. Blacky's howls suddenly ended, as if a stop button had been punched. I tucked myself into a fork in the branches and looked through a gap in the leaves.

Perfect. It was unlikely I would be seen from below. You would have to make a special effort to peer into the branches and there'd be no reason to do that. I unclipped my digital camera from the belt of my shorts – the same camera I'd taken along for the croc cruise – and looked through the viewfinder. It wasn't a top quality camera. The zoom function was, to be honest, crap. But, at this distance, I was confident I would get a picture of Murray that would be recognisable, that might hold up in a court of law. I turned the camera on and waited.

The men had gone into the bush a few metres, trying to track the source of the howling. Now they returned.

'What the hell *was* that?' asked one.

Murray shrugged.

'No idea, mate,' he said. 'Never heard a sound like that before. But I reckon we should get this carcass in the back of the ute and call it a day. I've got a special project on tomorrow. A really big croc. Over five metres. The top dog in the entire area. Capone, they call him. I'll meet you at nine.'

The men placed their rifles back against the side of the ute. I was pleased to note the guns could be clearly seen in the camera viewfinder. Then the guys bent down to lug the crocodile skin the remaining metre or so to the ute tray.

I waited.

I waited until Murray turned his head to the side to judge the distance, his face almost front-on to my lens. Then I clicked the shutter.

It was a great photo. The image appeared immediately on the small LCD screen and I knew at once that this was game, set and match. The butchered croc was easily identifiable. So was Murray, his hands gripping the corpse. The rifles were there. Even the ute's rego.

The entire operation was perfect in design and execution.

Apart from one slight detail.

You see, as I examined the photo, I slipped and crashed through the branches onto the soggy ground, like a piece of exotic fruit. Dylan and I seemed to be making a habit of this kind of thing, but at least Dyl had fallen into water.

The ground punched the air from my lungs. I struggled to my feet as Murray and the other two men walked quickly towards me. They didn't seem thrilled.

I had three chances, I thought, of getting out of this. One, their limbs might suddenly start to drop off. Two, a snake could bite them. Three, a croc could eat them.

When they stopped in front of me I had to admit that these had all been very long shots. So I tried a bright and cheery smile instead.

'Hi guys,' I said. 'Surprise! Just thought I'd drop in and see how you're going.'

One of the men scrunched up his fist in my T-shirt and pulled me close. I was terrified but determined not to show it.

'My mum ironed this shirt this morning,' I said. 'She is not going to be happy with you if it comes back creased.'

'Let him go, Mick,' said Murray. His voice was soft.

'He's been spying on us,' snarled Mick. His beard was very impressive in close-up. Not so his teeth, which were chipped and yellow. His eyes were simply hard. 'Taking photographs.'

'I said let him go, Mick.' Murray hadn't raised his voice, but it had authority. It reminded me of parents. They didn't yell, but you just *knew* you'd better do as instructed. Mick let go.

'Finish up in the ute,' Murray continued. 'I'll deal with this.'

The others slunk off, grumbling. Occasionally they looked back at me, as if imagining what they'd like to do if Murray wasn't around. I made a mental note not to invite them to

my next birthday party. If I lived to enjoy it.

Murray crouched in front of me. I put the camera behind my back and added another name to my birthday party exclusion list.

'No one's going to hurt you, Marcus,' he said. 'It *is* Marcus, isn't it?' I didn't reply. 'In fact, I'll take you back to the resort myself. But … you *do* understand, don't you? I can't let you keep the pictures in that camera. I simply can't allow it.'

'Sorry,' I replied. I was pleased to note my voice sounded strong and confident. 'But this is *my* camera and *my* pictures. If you're going to take them, then I guess you *will* have to hurt me.'

Murray sighed and rubbed a hand across the top of his head.

'I don't want to do that.'

'But you're good at it,' I said. I nodded towards the ute where the bearded thugs were tying down what remained of the croc. 'Isn't that part of the fun? Hurting things weaker than you? Hey, I'm eleven years old and a twentieth your size. Should be easy.'

'That crocodile is not weaker than me,' said Murray.

'In a swimming pool, that would be true,' I replied. 'But you had a gun. I'm guessing the croc didn't. Under those circumstances, I reckon you were in a slightly stronger position.'

Murray fixed me with his piercing blue eyes.

'You don't understand,' he said.

'That's true. I don't.'

'Marcus, I just want to delete those photographs. Then you

86

get the camera back and I take you home. End of story.'

'I'll tell everyone what I've seen.'

'Fair enough. And maybe some might take the word of an eleven-year-old kid against a forty-year-old doctor who's spent his life healing children. But you won't have *evidence* and that's the only thing of importance to me.' He smiled. This time I didn't like his smile. 'Come on, mate. You can't win this. Just hand over the camera, like a good boy.'

And suddenly another voice – one in my head – also told me to be a good boy. It explained why. Now *I* smiled. I took my hand from behind my back and held out the camera to Murray. His eyes softened as he reached out to take it.

I knew Blacky could move quickly. I'd seen his spectacular disappearing acts. But this time he outdid himself. He was a dirty-white streak as he launched himself between Murray and me, a blur, a haze, a smudge, a smear across the eyeballs. Before you even knew he was there, he was gone.

And so was my camera, wedged firmly in his jaws.

For a moment, Murray was too shocked to move. We stared at each other for a heartbeat or two. Then came confusion. There were shouts, yells and three men running after a small, dirty-white dog as it ducked and bobbed through the bush. It was unlikely they'd catch him.

I ran in the opposite direction.

Blacky met up with me twenty minutes later. He said he'd left Murray and the other two in the middle of a *very* wet and *very* smelly marsh. I clipped the camera back onto the waistband of my shorts and we headed back to the resort.

It had been quite an adventure and I was looking forward

to telling Dyl all about it. I was also looking forward to a rest.

You couldn't call this holiday dull. We'd been here less than twenty-four hours and Dyl had nearly been eaten by a crocodile and I'd completed the mission Blacky set. Once that camera and the evidence it contained was safely secured, there was no way Murray was going to get away with any more killing. True, we were leaving soon and I couldn't think how to avoid that. But I was pleased I'd achieved something important before the holiday was over.

But it *wasn't* over. It turned out the adventure hadn't finished with any of us yet. Not by a long chalk.

I watched as Brendan locked the camera into the safe behind the desk at reception. Only when he turned the key did I give a sigh of satisfaction. I didn't know if Murray would come back to the resort at all. Maybe he'd make a run for it. It didn't matter. Once I got the photographs into the hands of the police or the Parks and Wildlife authority, there wouldn't be anywhere for him to hide. It's not as if he was a nobody. He was a big man – in every sense of the word – with an important job. He'd be easy to find.

So it was with a spring in my step that I walked back to the cabin.

I didn't make it there unscathed.

Rose leaped out from a shrub at the side of the path, dragged me off into low-lying bush, clamped my head under her arm and gave my skull a good going-over with her knuckles.

'I hate you, Mucus,' she screamed. 'I really hate you.'

89

'What have I done?' I managed to croak. I was tired, dirty and hungry. I could have happily given up being tortured by an evil sibling at that particular moment.

'Ruined this holiday, that's what you've done. And I *told* you. I told you that if you messed this up I'd make you wish you had never been born.'

It's difficult to organise your thoughts when your head is being held in a vice and your brain feels as though it's being eaten by fire ants. I tried to throw up over Rose's shoes, but couldn't manage. I vowed to work on this. It would be very useful to be able to summon vomit at will.

'How have I ruined the holiday?' I gasped.

'The crocodile, Mucus? *Hello*?' She scarcely paused in the rhythm of her knuckle-grinding.

'That wasn't my fault. Even you said it wasn't my fault. An accident. That's what you said.'

'I was lying. It *is* your fault. That splat of cat poo is *your* friend. And he's a moron, an imbecile, a half-wit thicko and a brain-dead drongo. Falling off a boat! And now we all have to go home because of him. It's not fair, Mucus. You're responsible and you're going to pay.'

Her knuckles picked up pace. At this rate I'd be as bald as Murray by the time I was fourteen. For all that, I was impressed by her range of insults. Rose might be the devil's spawn, but she's got word power.

I screamed louder. With any luck, my wails would attract the attention of Mum and Dad. Maybe Rose thought the same, because she suddenly stopped her torture and let go of my head. I stood up, my hands holding the top of my skull. It felt like it was about to explode.

'I hate you, Mucus,' she said again. But her voice broke and I could tell she was crying. If I'd had time, I'd have made some guesses why. And probably most of those guesses would have involved Brendan, the chick-magnet waiter and croc-tour guide. But I wasn't about to look a gift horse in the mouth. I legged it for the cabin door. And made it safely.

Dylan was slurping a can of cola, watching television and looking bored.

I studied him closely for signs of delayed shock, but he seemed the same as always. What was it the doctor had said? *The mind takes time to catch up*. But maybe that was Dyl's strength. He lived entirely in the moment. The past and the future were different countries. For Dyl, the mind would probably never catch up.

'How you doing?' I asked.

'Ah, mate,' he said. 'Top quality. But bored as. I need to get out of here. Reckon your mum will let me?'

'Probably,' I replied. A thought struck me. 'Since when did you worry about getting permission from anyone?'

Dyl looked slightly embarrassed.

'She's all right, your mum. I don't wanna … you know … worry her or anything. Anyway, where have you been, Marc? I've been waiting, watching dumb soap operas and you've been gone for hours.'

It occurred to me then that Dylan had missed a lot of action since his attempt at synchronised swimming with a man-eating croc. He didn't know about the holiday being cut short. He didn't know what had happened with Murray. It was time to fill him in.

'Do you want the good news or the bad news?' I said.

'Good news.'

So I told him how Blacky and I had stalked Murray in the bush, got the incriminating evidence, managed a daredevil escape. I got right into it, living the excitement and danger all over again. I was gabbling. But the more I talked the longer Dylan's face grew. When I got to putting the camera in the safe, I thought he was going to burst into tears. He turned away from me.

'What's up, mate?' I said.

'Oh, man!' I don't think I had ever heard so much pain in his voice before. 'That sucks. That really, really sucks. You call this *good* news?'

'I don't get it.' I didn't, though I should have.

'You're off having fun, Marc. Danger, excitement. Completing the mission. And I *missed* it. I'm sitting here watching *The Young and the Dumb* or *The Old and the Senile* or whatever it's called, and all the time you're having an adventure. Without me.'

I felt bad for him and annoyed with myself. I should have known he'd react that way. Dylan lives for danger. I was tempted to point out that dive-bombing a croc was enough daily excitement for a normal person. Luckily, I stopped myself. Dyl isn't a normal person.

I hadn't got to the bad news yet. Maybe I'd leave telling him for a while. He'd almost certainly forget to ask.

'What's the bad news, then?'

I told him.

'Whaaat?' he yelled. 'They can't do that. I don't want to go home, Marc. Tell them.'

'I think it's too late, mate. Their minds are made up. They're worried about how your parents are going to react when they hear you nearly disappeared down a croc's throat.'

'Mum and Dad will be okay with it. It's happened before.'

'What?' Even though I know Dylan well and nothing about him really surprises me, I found it hard to believe this was an experience he went through with monotonous regularity. 'So just how often do you have a close encounter with a saltwater croc, then, Dyl?'

He waved his arms dismissively.

'Not with a croc. But brushes with death? Loads. Like the time I used Dad's blowtorch to dry my shorts and set the house on fire. Or the time I kept a Western Brown snake in my bedside cupboard. Or the time ...'

'Okay, Dyl,' I said. 'I get the message. But my olds are not your olds. They don't realise that swimming with man-eating crocs is just part and parcel of the Dylan Smith experience.'

'I'll go and tell them.'

And he was up and out the door before I could stop him. I supposed it wouldn't hurt if he had a word. But I wasn't optimistic. In fact, I was downright depressed. The thrill of completing the mission was fading rapidly.

I turned back to switch off the television and there was Blacky, sitting on my bed and sniffing at his bum.

'Who said the mission was finished, tosh?' came the voice in my head. 'Certainly not me.'

'But ...'

'*Half*-done, mush. The best bit's yet to come.'

'I don't get it, Blacky,' I said. 'We caught the serial killer red-handed. What else is there to do?'

''Fraid I can't tell you that, bucko.'

'So, what then? It's a secret? Or am I meant to guess? Perhaps we could play charades? Six syllables, sounds like "A complete waste of time"!'

'You have a nasty tendency towards sarcasm, mush. It's not attractive.'

I sighed and swallowed my frustration.

'Help me here, Blacky.'

'There's an animal who wants to tell you himself. In fact, he insists on it. A personal meeting.'

'And who's the animal?'

'Friendly guy. Australian icon. Much misunderstood.'

I was getting a bad feeling about this.

'The animal, Blacky?'

I think this was the first time I saw the dog look uncomfortable. He made a big deal of examining his bum, scratching around his hindquarters and giving himself a brisk shake.

I kept the question looping in my mind.

'You know him as Al,' said Blacky eventually. And reluctantly. Then it all fell into place.

'Al?' I said. I almost felt like laughing. 'Al Capone, the humungous saltwater crocodile? Al, the killing machine? Al, the dude who very nearly snacked on Dyl?'

'That's not a very flattering portrait, tosh. Be fair.'

'Are you completely out of your mind, Blacky? Forget it. Tell Al to forget it. Thank him for his kind invitation but tell him I'm busy. Tell him I'm washing my hair. No chance, *bucko*. Zilch, *tosh*. Thanks, but no thanks, *boyo*.'

'You thought he was beautiful. Out there in the bush. I read your mind.'

'So's a volcano. Doesn't mean I'm going to stick my head down one.'

'Al won't like it,' said Blacky.

'Frankly, I don't care if he has a hissy fit, spits the dummy bigtime and throws himself on the ground in a temper tantrum. There's no way I'm going near that thing. Tell him to text me. Or, if he wants to talk, then *you* go see him. Take messages back and forth. There you go. Everyone happy.'

'Won't work,' said Blacky. 'He wants to see you personally. He was very clear about that.'

'I hope he'll be able to live with the disappointment.'

'You need to think about this, tosh,' said Blacky. 'It really isn't a good idea to turn Al down. He's used to getting his own way. If you won't go to him, he might decide to come to you. I don't think you'd like that.'

'Well, Blacky,' I said. 'He's welcome to try. But I'm locking

95

that door, so he'll either need a master key or a set of lock picks. I doubt sliding a credit card down the mechanism is going to get him very far. Then there's the small detail about turning the knob with stubby arms that I suspect weren't designed for that purpose. However,' – I waved my own arms about – 'if he gets through all of that, I'll make a pot of tea and get out the lamingtons.'

'You owe him,' said Blacky. 'And you owe me.'

'I'm sorry?'

'He had your mate on toast. There, in the water. If it wasn't for me, Dylan would be passing through Al's lower intestines right now.'

That small fragment of memory came into my head. Dylan's head in the water, the crocodile's snout behind him and, way off in the distance, on the river bank, a dirty-white shape that flashed in and out of existence. I didn't have to say anything.

'That's right, tosh,' said Blacky. 'I put in a word. Told Al it would a good thing to pass on lunch. That you would be grateful. And it's not easy for a five-and-a-half-metre saltie to suddenly adopt a calorie-controlled diet when something small and tasty is dangling there, asking to be eaten. Like I said, you owe him and you owe me.'

Suddenly, going home lost its terrors. I mean, it had been good enough for all other Christmases. Presents under the tree. Mum's roast turkey (provided it was a volunteer). And virtually no chance of stumbling across a five-metre saltwater crocodile …

I didn't get much chance to think this through because the door suddenly opened. I half expected to see Al standing there with an uzi submachine gun and a bottle of chianti. But it was Dyl and Dad.

I could tell by the expression on Dyl's face that his pleas had done no good.

I glanced over to my bed, but Blacky had vanished. Again. I was beginning to suspect that he'd stolen Harry Potter's invisibility cloak.

Dad sat on the edge of Dyl's bed.

'Sorry, boys,' he said. 'But there is a flight late tomorrow and we are going to be on it. This is not something we have decided without careful thought. At least we'll be home by Christmas. And Dylan is welcome to spend it at our house, if his parents agree.'

I could tell Dad was genuinely upset. And it was good of him to offer to have Dylan around. Not many people who weren't in secure psychiatric hospitals, drooling and trying to eat the carpet, would do that.

But it didn't lighten our mood. Me, Dad and Dyl sat around for a while, but in the end we had nothing to say to each other.

It was a gloomy gathering for dinner that evening. True, Rose and Cy had made an effort. In fact, it seemed they were auditioning for *Australia's Top Model* and *Extreme Makeover Disasters* at the same time. It was scary. Their make-up the previous evening had been over the top. Tonight it was in orbit. Both wore dresses made of lace, ribbons and meringue, their hair piled up on their heads like lacquered elephant dung. A force 5 cyclone couldn't have shifted one hair out of place.

They completely ignored each other. Whenever someone else spoke, they grunted. Seems the effort they made was limited to appearance.

Dyl and I weren't a barrel of laughs either. I hadn't mentioned what Blacky had said about the mission being half over. As far as I was concerned I had done enough. I didn't need to risk sliding down a croc's throat like a human-flavoured M&M. But Dyl wouldn't see it like that. This new task could be his only chance to experience a bit of excitement. I felt guilty. But it was wiser to say nothing.

Dad tried to be cheerful, but he wasn't fooling anyone. Mum made a point of beaming at everyone, particularly Dylan. It was beginning to spook me out, particularly when he smiled back. Then she turned her beam around the restaurant. It was like watching a human lighthouse.

'That poor man is eating by himself again,' she trilled. 'I think we should invite him to our table. What do you say, gang?'

'Good idea, love,' said Dad. 'I'll ask him to join us.'

I looked over to see who they were talking about and realised Murray *had* returned. My heart jumped. He sat at the same table as last night and as far as I could tell he didn't have a care in the world.

'Dad, no!' I said. 'He's a ...'

'Come on, son,' replied Dad. 'Have a little charity. He looks lonely.' And he was out of his chair before I could say anything more. Dyl and I glanced at each other. This could be awkward. Then again, I reckoned I'd be the last person Murray would want to sit with. No chance he'd say yes.

Right again, Marcus, I thought as Murray stood, picked up his glass and followed Dad back to our table. *It's such a burden always being right.*

Dad did the introductions. Mum was thrilled to discover Murray was a Consultant Paediatrician. She almost curtsied, which is difficult when you're sitting down. Rose and Cy were less impressed. They grunted. It was as if they were competitors for the title of World's Worst-Dressed Pig Impersonator.

Murray smiled as he shook my hand and then Dyl's.

'I've already met your sons, Mrs Hill,' he said. 'It was quite an experience.'

'Why, thank you, Dr Small,' Mum replied. I would have put money on Mum throwing a fit if anyone suggested she was responsible for Dyl's gene pool. But she didn't bat an eyelid. Murray ran a hand across the top of his head.

'It's actually Mr Small,' he said. 'Consultants are called Mr. But I would much prefer it if you called me Murray.'

'Mr Small,' I said. 'Isn't that a character from a kids' picture book? You know. Mr Small, Mr Greedy … Mr Mean?'

Murray smiled.

'Quite right, mate,' he said.

He sat between me and Dyl and insisted on buying drinks for all of us. I turned him down. So did Dyl. For the first time in his life he passed on a cola! I would have taken a picture, if I'd had a camera. Murray snapped his fingers, and Brendan came over to take the order.

Rose and Cy reacted as though they'd been zapped with tasers. They went from multi-coloured mounds of misery to sickeningly chirpy in less than a second.

'Hi, Brendan,' said Cy. She dragged out all the syllables of this imaginative greeting. It seemed to go on for thirty seconds. 'How *are* you?' she added, thus clinching her status of inspirational conversationalist.

'Hi,' said Brendan. 'Can I get you guys some drinks before you order food?'

'Please,' said Murray. 'We'd like a bottle of ...'

'Brendan, I think what you did this morning was the bravest thing I have *ever* seen!' This was Rose. 'Battling a crocodile to save the life of *poor* Dylan here. You deserve a *medal*.'

Brendan shifted from one foot to the other and scratched behind an ear. The resulting draught nearly knocked me off my chair.

'Well, not sure "battling" is the right word. I just helped to pull the kid out.'

'We'll go for the bottle of ...' said Murray.

'How *modest*!' simpered Cy, batting her eyelashes in Brendan's direction. Given she was wearing very long false ones, he almost toppled over in the breeze. I was beginning to think we didn't need ceiling fans, when Rose harrumphed and knocked a glass of iced water into Cy's lap. Cy screamed as she jumped to her feet.

Murray took advantage of the confusion to order a bottle of champagne. I sneaked a peek at the wine list. It cost $190.

Cy gave Rose a look designed to turn her into stone. Then she rushed off to change and peace reigned for a while.

'What do you want for Christmas?' Murray whispered to me.

'A healthy environment,' I whispered back.

'Tricky to wrap.'

'But worth the effort.'

Murray took a sip of champagne while I toyed with the idea of knocking a glass of iced water into his lap. I didn't, though. I refuse to imitate Rose, even when she comes up with a brilliant idea.

'I reckon a boy like you might really appreciate a new computer,' Murray said after a long pause. 'Possibly the latest games console as well. Plus games. A mobile phone, maybe. What do you think, Marcus? Would you like those things for Christmas?'

'Nah,' I said. 'Too expensive.'

'Not necessarily.'

'Yes,' I said. 'Necessarily.'

'There must be something you'd like.'

I thought about this.

'There is, actually,' I replied. 'There's one thing you can do for me.'

And I told him.

Dylan and I watched TV, but we weren't really paying attention.

Dyl had scarcely said a word all evening. He hadn't even smiled when Rose and Cy got stuck into each other during dinner. And it was quite a performance. Whenever Brendan was around they oozed happiness and joy from every pore. As soon as he left, it was as if someone had turned off the tap of wellbeing. They sank into misery, punctuated by occasional moments of outright nastiness.

Eventually, they became so bitchy that Mum sent them back to their cabins.

Dyl and I could hear them yelling at each other over the sound of the TV. We had to crank up the volume. But I *felt* the slam of their cabin door. It was a minor earthquake. Maybe Cy was making her getaway. Maybe Rose had taken to Cy's head with her knuckles and got disembowelled by a thrust from a light sabre. Serve her right.

We must have dozed off for a couple of hours, because the next thing I was aware of was a hammering at our cabin door. I got to my feet and glanced at the alarm clock. It was past midnight. Dyl sat up in bed, blinking his eyes and looking groggy. I staggered to the door.

'Who is it?' I called.

I didn't want to open up. I remembered what Blacky had said about Al paying a visit. For all I knew, a mob of crocs could be outside with broad-brimmed hats, sawn-off shotguns and bad accents.

'It's Dad,' came a muffled voice. 'Open the door, son.'

I did. It wasn't just Dad. Mum was there. So was Rose, Brendan and his father, Ted, the resort manager. They glanced past me into our room.

'Is Siobhan here?' asked Mum.

Had she lost her mind? Cy in our cabin? I'd sooner entertain a five-metre croc. I shook my head.

'What's up?' I asked.

'She's gone,' said Mum, almost choking on the words. 'Siobhan has disappeared.'

Apparently, Cy had taken off after my sensitive sister had pointed out a few of her character flaws. Such as:

* She didn't have a character
* She was as attractive as a pitbull terrier's backside
* She couldn't pull a muscle, let alone a guy like Brendan.

I had to read between the lines to get this information.

Anyway, after a couple of hours, Rose decided to look for her, possibly because she had thought up a few more insults and wanted to share them. But Cy was nowhere to be found. Rose alerted our parents who, in turn, sought out Brendan as the likely person Cy would run to. He hadn't seen her. He and Ted searched the entire resort and turned up nothing. Finally they came to our cabin.

Now only one place remained.

The bush.

And it was past midnight.

Mum hadn't recovered from Dyl's dip with Al. Now she had to face the prospect that yet another person's child

was in serious danger. Judging by the look on her face, she realised she'd blown her chance of being nominated Responsible Guardian of the Year.

We searched the resort again. It gave us something to do, rather than follow Mum's lead of slumping in a chair, moaning 'Oh my God' and smacking herself around the head with a heavy palm leaf. Okay, I'm exaggerating. But only just. By the time we'd finished it was one-twenty-seven and Cy still hadn't been found.

Ted gazed into the bush.

'We can't go in there,' he said. 'It's too dark. Anyway, I reckon she's probably only a couple of metres in, trying to scare us all. You know, making someone pay because she's upset. With luck, she'll get tired and come back soon. No worries.'

But she didn't. When dawn arrived, the resort was stubbornly Cy-less.

Worries.

Search parties were organised at first light. Most of the holiday-makers volunteered to help and Ted Branaghan divided people into groups and gave them areas to search. I noticed Murray poring over maps. Dyl and I joined the queue of volunteers, but Mum dragged us out.

'You are NOT going,' she said. 'I will not risk it. From now on, Marcus, you will be chained to your bedpost until you are forty. Possibly forty-five.'

'But we want to help, Mrs Hill,' said Dyl. He was close to tears. All this sitting around was driving him crazy. Around sixty cans of cola bubbled and fizzed in his system and the sugar was demanding release.

'I know you want to help, Dylan,' she said. 'Which is why I need you to stay here and watch in case Siobhan comes back.'

We argued, but it did no good. Mum wasn't so much firm as set in quick-drying cement. So Dyl and I slouched off to sit on the edge of the swimming pool.

'Man, this sucks the big one,' said Dylan. If anything, the darkness of his mood had deepened. I agreed, but what could we do? I stuck my feet into the water, made small waves and watched them break against the poolside. Part of me hoped Cy wouldn't be discovered until the flight this evening had left. Though, on reflection, even if we missed the flight, we'd be off home as soon as Cy turned up. Dyl *and* Cy in danger? We'd shoot through even if Mum and Dad had to hire pushbikes or hijack a passing camel train.

'I know where she is.'

In all the drama I'd forgotten about Blacky. I was so surprised by the voice I nearly fell into the pool. He was sitting on the diving board. I got the sudden urge to see him attempt a half-turn with pike, but thrust the thought to one side.

'You know where Cy is?'

'Sure do, tosh. I think I already mentioned that there is little that goes on in this world of which I am unaware. She's fine, but needs your help. If you'll follow me ...'

'But Mum said we've got to stay here, Blacky. Can't I just tell one of the search parties and they could follow you?'

'Oh, I see, mush. "This dog told me where the missing person is. Kindly follow him. This is a Disney movie!" And

how about an encore, bucko? "I'm also in email contact with a small dingo called Ernie." That should guarantee you a fitting for a straitjacket.'

I could see his point. I told Dyl what was going on. Perhaps he could figure a way out of the problem.

He could.

'Let's go, Marcus,' he yelled, already scrabbling at the lock on the pool gate. I sighed and followed. I'd just have to put up with Mum's anger later. And – maybe – finding Cy would the best defence against it.

Maybe.

After half an hour of following Blacky through the bush, I was completely lost. Actually, I was lost within two minutes. There's something about the bush that makes it difficult to get your bearings. It's probably to do with how the landscape doesn't change. Mangrove trees, palms with sharp, spiky leaves that trail the ground, marshy ground punctuated by pools of water. Get through that and exactly the same is in front. It's like walking the wrong way on an escalator. Your legs keep moving, but the scenery doesn't alter.

'How much further, Blacky?' I called.

'Nearly there, tosh.'

Dyl and I made our way around a mass of mangrove roots and suddenly found ourselves in a clearing. The water was deeper here. In fact, small hummocks of earth poked, like islands, above the waterline. This was not friendly country. Without wading up to our waists in brackish water there appeared to be no way through. I thought about those limb-chomping bugs Blacky had mentioned. They were probably

gathered here in gangs, rubbing their hands in anticipation and getting dibs on particular arms and legs.

On that cheerful note I spotted Cy.

She sat on one of the islands, thirty or forty metres away, staring straight ahead. Motionless.

'Cy!' I yelled. I waved my arms above my head.

She gave not even the slightest sign of having seen or heard me.

'Siobhan!' I tried. In the past she'd refused to respond to Cy, though I thought it unlikely she'd be quite so fussy under these circumstances. Still nothing. Dyl and I glanced at each other. There was no choice. Bugs or no bugs, we waded towards her.

At least we made it with all eight limbs attached.

I knelt in the mud beside Cy. She still hadn't made a movement. Her eyes stared blankly ahead. I tried waving my hands in front of her face. She didn't so much as blink. When I pushed against her arm, she rocked slightly like one of those toys with a weight in the bottom, and then went back to staring at something beyond my vision. To be honest, it was spooky.

Cy was a mess physically as well. Her clothes were soaking and her face was streaked with mud. The elephant-dung hair-do had come unravelled and fell in clotted strips around her face. But it was her eyes that worried me most. They were glazed, blank, as if no one was home.

'What are we going to do, Dyl?' I said.

'Get help, mate,' said Dyl. 'I don't fancy our chances of carrying her. What *is* that hound barking at?'

I hadn't noticed Blacky's absence. He was off somewhere

to our left, barking like a mad thing. We turned in that direction and saw him swimming towards us. Twenty metres behind came Murray Small.

Help had arrived, though it wasn't the help I would have chosen under ideal circumstances.

Murray took over immediately. As he was an adult and a child doctor, I supposed that was fair enough.

He took Cy's pulse. He peeled back an eyelid and stared into one unseeing orb. Dyl, Blacky and I waited. Finally, Murray turned towards us.

'Her vital signs are good,' he said. 'But she's in shock and suffering from exposure. We need to get her back immediately.' He held her hand. I noticed that he stroked it gently with his thumb. 'But I don't really understand. Spending all night out here must have been dreadful, but it shouldn't account for this condition. The girl is catatonic.' He noticed our puzzled expressions. 'Almost paralysed, as if the mind has shut down the body,' he explained. 'What I don't understand is the fear that produced this reaction.'

'Ah. I might be able to help you out with that,' said Dyl.

We eyed him expectantly.

'Behind you,' he said.

Murray and I turned.

Murray's eyes probably came out – *boiiing* – on stalks. I know mine did. I didn't check for synchronised eye-popping because one thing held all my attention. Actually, seven things.

Saltwater crocodiles. Six huge crocs, advancing slowly towards us – and another that wasn't so much huge as

monstrous. They fanned out until we were surrounded. The largest slithered up onto the mound where we stood and stopped a couple of metres away. No one made a sound. I think all of us would have *liked* to scream, but terror had stolen our breath.

'Allow me to make the introductions,' came Blacky's voice in my head. 'Al, this is Marcus. Marcus, Al. I think you have already met his drongo sidekick, Dylan. Oh, and the humungous slaphead is Murray. The guy who shot your brother.'

'Incidentally, tosh,' said Blacky. 'You might be interested to know that it's not only killers like Murray who are a threat to Al and his mates. The cane toad, introduced to this country by humans, remember, is poisoning many animals in its relentless march across the Territory ...'

'Blacky,' I yelled in my head. 'Spare me the environmental sermon, man. I am just about to be eaten by a crocodile and I don't want the last words I ever hear to be your drivel. All I want, frankly, is to give you one last vicious kick up the bum.'

'Charming,' he replied, all offended.

If I had had time or energy, I'd have taken him to task about his attitude. *He* was offended? *He* was sulky? I mean, we had followed him in good faith and this was our reward? To be the special on the crocodile menu? Humans on toast. Marinated in a tasty sweat sauce. I only hoped they would have room afterwards for a dessert of flatulent dog. Because a penny had dropped. He *knew* why Cy was petrified with fear. He *knew* the crocs had been waiting

for us. Blacky had led us into a trap.

His silence confirmed my suspicions.

I flicked my eyes away from Al. Murray and Dyl hadn't budged. Cy looked as though she'd never budge again. Now all of us were paralysed by fear. If the others were like me, they *wanted* to run and scream and probably poop their pants, but their bodies had gone into shut-down mode. I felt particularly bad for Dyl. Just how unlucky was he? It's not many people who survive a swim with a croc, only to be eaten by the same croc the following day. More proof, I guess, that Dyl is a disaster magnet.

I didn't give Murray more than a fleeting thought. Partly because there was a poetic justice in his probable end, but mainly because I was too worried about myself. I hadn't been on this earth long. I wasn't keen to leave it while I had still so much life to live and so much to do.

'Al isn't going to eat you,' said Blacky. 'I already told you this, tosh. He just wants to talk. And if you'd agreed when I'd first asked, then he wouldn't have had to set this up. Of course, your sister's friend here made it easier by providing herself as bait. But in the end, all this is your fault, mush.'

'Whaaat?' I was really tempted to argue. *My* fault? Of course. How silly I'd been, not wanting to be alone with a five-metre man-eating saltwater crocodile. Only got myself to blame! But then Blacky's first words registered.

'Are you sure he's not going to eat us?'

'Well, he *said* he's not going to eat you and me, tosh. I can't answer for the others, but if I was Murray I wouldn't be planning to read any long books.'

'Then tell him the only way I'll talk is if he lets everyone else go. And what do you mean, "he *said*"?'

Blacky sighed.

'He's a croc, boyo, not a Tibetan monk. I don't think we can be a hundred per cent certain he always keeps his word.'

That was comforting. But it didn't alter things. I suppose I didn't have much more to lose. If Al really wanted to talk, then he would have to agree to my terms. He obviously needed something from me and maybe I could make him pay a price for that. Or maybe he'd eat all of us, which was probably what was going to happen anyway. And, listen, it wasn't me being a hero, like everyone said later. I just thought it was a waste of life. True, I might have negotiated that only Murray got eaten. You could argue the world would have been a better place. But for me it was all or nothing.

'Tell him, Blacky,' I said. 'The others leave. I stay. And then we talk. If not, he won't get a peep out of me. This is non-negotiable.'

'I'll tell him, tosh. But before I do, think this through. If he agrees, what are you going to say to your serial-killer mate? "Don't worry, I've struck a deal with the head honcho. You can toddle along while I chew the fat for a while?"'

He had a point. I could tell Dyl, but Murray was a different matter. It was unlikely he'd pick up Cy and wander off, secure in the knowledge an eleven-year-old kid had nego-tiated safe passage with an estuarine croc. As it turned out, Murray solved the problem for me.

'Marcus,' he hissed. 'Listen to me. Listen closely. I have a plan. It might not work, but it's the best I can come up

with. When I shout "Now" I want you and Dylan to grab Siobhan. Pick her up. And run. As fast as you can.'

'And this will help, how?' I asked.

'I am going to attack the crocodiles, draw them away from you. With luck, they will all go for me and give you guys a chance.'

It wasn't much of a chance. Murray knew it. I knew it.

'So you are going to sacrifice yourself for us?'

'I'm a doctor,' he said. 'I have spent my adult life saving children. Anyway, as I'm sure you, of all people, understand, there's a kind of irony in this.' He tried to smile but it came out wrong. Twisted. 'From the hunter to the hunted. Maybe it's what I deserve.'

'Okay,' I said. 'Just give me a moment to get my head around this.'

'Tell Al my conditions, Blacky,' I thought. 'And tell him I am not prepared to bargain.' The answer came almost immediately.

'Al agrees,' said Blacky. 'He says he admires your guts.'

'Tell him he's welcome to, provided he admires them from a distance.'

I whispered into Dyl's ear, explained what I was going to do. 'Help Murray get her out of here,' I added. Dyl nodded. I instructed Blacky to pass the plan on to Al. Now I could only hope. And trust that the word of a crocodile was worth more than the word of many a human.

'Okay, Murray,' I said. 'Let's go for this. Count down from ten. When you get to zero, we'll grab Cy and make a run for it. Ready?'

Murray was petrified. Who could blame him? His eyes

filled with tears and his whole body shook. But he didn't stop rubbing Cy's hand, even as he stared at the crocs surrounding us.

'I'm not all bad, Marcus,' he said. 'I want you to know that. You would have got your Christmas present.'

'No one's all bad,' I said. 'Or all good. But we need to keep that bad side in check.'

He just nodded.

'Ten,' he said, and his voice was shaky. 'Nine, eight, seven, six.' His voice became stronger as the countdown continued and he stopped trembling. 'Five, four ...'

And on four, I jumped to my feet and ran.

I splashed through water, waving my arms and yelling. I kept my eyes fixed firmly on the next mound, about thirty metres away. I was terrified, I have to admit. At any moment I expected to feel a jaw clamp down on my leg, sharp teeth slicing through skin and muscle. Even above my own noise, I could hear the slither and splash as the reptiles followed. Out of the corner of one eye I could see a couple of the crocs flanking me, their cold eyes fixed upon mine.

It was the longest thirty metres of my life.

When I finally clambered up onto the bank, tired, stressed and sopping wet, I was amazed by two things. One, that I was still alive and two, that Dylan was right on my heels.

'Yo, Marc,' he said, pulling a can of cola from his ridiculous jacket and popping the ring-pull. 'Wassup, dude?'

I slumped down into the mud. I had to catch my breath.

'Dyl, ya dill,' I panted. 'What the hell are you doing? You were supposed to stay, you moron. That's why I was creating the diversion. To give you all the chance to escape.'

Dylan sat down and took a long slurp from his can. He wore an offended expression.

'Yeah, I know what I was *meant* to do,' he said. 'But we are buddies, Marc. You and me. Like last time. Partners on a mission. Fatman and Robin. And I wasn't going to miss out *again*. This is unbelievably cool.'

I wished I could have shared his sentiments. I watched as the circle of crocs closed in once again and I was glad Dylan was with me.

It may have been selfish, but I was glad.

Murray hadn't moved. He was staring at us. The distance was too great to be entirely sure, but I think his bottom jaw was scraping his boots. I waved.

'Get Cy out of here,' I yelled. 'And get help.'

I'd left him with no option. He made as if to move towards us, but then his shoulders slumped. He put Cy over one slumped shoulder and waded away. I had no idea how far it was to civilisation but I knew he'd be back. And that Cy was safe. We watched until he'd disappeared from sight.

I looked around. It was just the three of us, now. Me, Dyl and Blacky. Oh, and seven very large specimens of the most ruthless predator in the world.

'Wrong, bucko,' said Blacky. '*Homo sapiens* is, by a long distance, the most ruthless predator in the world.'

'Shut up, Blacky,' I said. 'Believe me, I am *not* in the mood.'

And what exactly did Dyl mean by Fatman?

Maybe I needed to lose weight.

Finally, the huge saltie spoke.

'Buongiorno,' said Al. 'I would kissa you, both cheeks, but is difficult, I think. Instead, I offer respect, my family to your family. I also offer food. Would be good, huh? Pasta and meatballs in ma special sauce. But this difficult, too. Howsabout a little bitta wild pig? Fresh kill.'

Look. I might have explained all this before, but I can't actually speak directly to other animals. I can only talk to Blacky. He, in turn, can communicate with a few other animals, Al apparently being one. So this conversation had to be channelled through Blacky. But it would be really tiring, not to mention boring, if I reported our three-way conversation as it actually happened. So, I'll just tell you what Al said as if he'd said it to me.

I turned down the kind offer of food. I wasn't hungry, but even if I had been, I didn't relish snacking on raw pig. I also felt this was not the best time to point out that I'd been tempted by the croc burger at the restaurant the day before yesterday. Knowing my luck, it would have been his mother and that would have blown all the family respect business.

'This my family,' continued Al. 'I do introductions. This brother and *consigliere* Guiseppe, other brother Paolo, sons Alfredo, Vito, Luigi and Rocco.'

Each croc, in turn, lifted a front leg in greeting. I gave small waves back, before I realised how ridiculous this was. Rocco the croc-o? I took a time-out with Blacky.

'What's with all the Mafia stuff?' I hissed. 'These are dinky-di Aussie animals. "G'day, mate, beaut, slap a prawn on the barbie and let's crack a cold one from the esky, no worries" I might have expected. Certainly not a bad imitation of *Goodfellas*.'

If Blacky could have shrugged, I dare say he would've.

'No idea, tosh,' he said. 'Maybe they've watched too many episodes of *The Sopranos*.'

'Blacky,' I said. '*The Sopranos*? What? On a forty-two inch plasma screen in their front room, while waiting for the pizza delivery guy to front up?'

'Okay. Maybe *I've* watched too many episodes of *The Sopranos*. But you've got to admit it is appropriate. These guys are pretty ruthless.'

'You are one sick puppy,' I said. 'No pun intended. And your sense of humour is similarly sick.'

So, too, his sense of geography, I thought. The Sopranos had American accents, not this cheap-Italian-pasta-sauce-commercial stereotype.

'Everyone's a critic these days,' said Blacky in a snotty tone.

I ignored him.

Mind you, I had to admit the Italian angle *was* fitting, though I'd die before I told Blacky. Then I remembered that I was probably going to die anyway. Then I remembered I couldn't keep my thoughts from Blacky in any case. He chuckled in my head. I hate that dog.

'I've gotta pee,' said Dylan.

'And how are you going to manage that, mate?' I asked. 'Ask if you can use their croc dunny?'

'Nah,' said Dyl. 'But I'm busting. I'll have to do it here. Just turn your back.'

'Dylan,' I replied, with more than a touch of exasperation in my voice. 'We have just gone through the whole business involving snack food. You whip anything out here, they're going to take it as an invitation to go for a cocktail sausage.'

Dylan mulled this over.

'I guess I could hold on,' he said.

Al had been patient during all this. Now he continued.

'My sons, here, they notta keen on talking,' he said. 'Rocco, he no like talk, talk, talk. He want action. Headstrong, like his Papa when I wassa his age.'

I had no idea which one was Rocco. All of them looked as though they were keen on action, especially if it involved chewing on human limbs. I kept quiet and tried to appear as if I was paying close attention. Which, to be honest, I was.

'But I amma still Head of da Family. I say, we needa make business legitimate. No more gang wars. No more taking outta da rival families in restaurant bloodbaths. Thatsa the past. The future? It abouta da lawyers and corporate meetings, not machine guns and garrottes.'

I sighed. Blacky didn't need me to say anything.

'Sorry, tosh,' he said. 'I'm just doing my best to keep him in character. Have you any idea how boring it is being a translator?'

'Fine,' I replied. 'Just don't make stuff up, all right? This is difficult enough as it is.'

It was slightly better after that. At least Al came to the point and I found out what the other half of the mission involved. Of course, that didn't mean I had any chance of completing it.

'Is he nuts, Blacky?' I said. 'Hang on. Do not pass on that thought! But let me get this clear. He wants me to stop the proposed government law that would allow big-game hunters to shoot crocs in the Northern Territory?' I remembered what Brendan had said on the croc cruise. Boy, that seemed a long time ago. He'd mentioned how trophy hunters were illegally killing crocodiles, but he'd also said something about the government allowing wealthy people to shoot them for sport. At a price.

'Tell him I'm sympathetic.' And I was. Of course I was. 'But I'm just a kid. I can't get my mum to change her mind, let alone a government.'

Al chewed this over.

'But thissa new world. Communication revolution. You use that.'

What was he talking about? I couldn't make it out. Anyway, this all seemed one-sided. What about crocodile attacks? If he was serious about finding a new way to live with human beings, shouldn't he reconsider his disturbing tendency to chow down on passing tourists?

'Hey. I act in good faith. This human I letta go, he kill. He kill my brother. No respect my family. But I let him go. Now *you* do something for *me*. Capisce?'

It was my turn to chew things over. I spotted a hidden threat in his words – not very well hidden, come to think of it – but Al *was* right. It must have taken a strong will to allow Murray to walk out of there. But I still couldn't see how to help. Blacky interrupted my thoughts.

'You're being a twonk, boyo. Yeah, crocs kill people. But think about it. You guys come into his territory, knowing his nature. You fish, you swim in his swimming holes. Some of you kill crocs to make shoes and handbags out of their skins. What do you expect from a wild animal when you mess around in his habitat? If you go to the zoo, you don't hop into the lion enclosure to enjoy a close-up. And, frankly, if you do then you've only got yourself to blame when it all goes belly-up. Or belly-ripped-up.'

'Yeah,' I said. 'I take your point. I just thought ...'

Blacky gave a snort of disgust.

'Tell you what, tosh. You find a saltwater croc in your front room watching tv or raiding your fridge for a bite to eat, you shoot him, okay? We'll call it quits. Until then, admit the injustice is all one-way.'

I scratched my head. Carefully. I didn't want anyone to misinterpret sudden movements.

'Okay, Blacky,' I said. 'This isn't the time to argue. But I still don't know what I can *do*. Write a stern letter to the newspaper?'

There was silence while we all thought. The crocodiles didn't move much, which was just as well. There were ten of us crowded on that hillock and you couldn't swing a cat. If I'd tried to swing a cat it would probably be more of a temptation than they could resist. So we sat quietly and gave the problem our full attention.

Then Blacky farted. Even the crocs moved back a little.

'For God's sake, Blacky,' I cried. 'I am not having fun here and this is about the last thing I need. Any more foul fumes from you and I'll be *asking* Al to eat me. At least it would be a quicker and more pleasant death.'

And that was when the idea came. It's not often a vile fart gives you blinding inspiration. A blinding headache, maybe. But Blacky couldn't take all the credit. Murray was owed some, too. Murray who, I noticed, had returned with help. My dad, Brendan and his dad, Ted, emerged from the bush onto the edge of the clearing about a hundred metres away.

They made an odd group: man-mountain Murray, Dad with his thin white legs, Brendan with his jug-handle ears and Ted with his torn singlet and stained stubbies. But I was *very* glad to see them.

They stopped when they saw us and I could almost read *their* thoughts. There was no cover to get any closer. Not without spooking the crocs. And no one wanted to spook the crocs.

Even at that distance I could see Dad carried himself like someone who had aged fifty years in five seconds.

He stood next to Ted Branaghan. Ted carried something long and thin. As I watched, he lifted it to his shoulder. There was a flash of sunlight on metal.

Ted lowered the rifle.

I knew what he was thinking. It was too dangerous to risk firing. For one thing, he might hit Dylan or me. For another, even if he managed to get one croc, there were six others who presumably might be stirred up a little by gunfire. He didn't want stirred-up crocs scurrying around anyone's ankles.

I stood and waved my arms. The four men cringed and waved their arms around in turn. It wasn't difficult to get the message. *Stay still*! Attracting attention, at least from their perspective, was the action of a moron. A soon-to-be-digested moron.

So we gazed at each other across an expanse of flooded land. This didn't seem to get us very far. Ted must have come to the same conclusion, because he cupped his hands around his mouth and yelled. 'Marcus! Keep very still and very quiet. I've radioed for help and it's on its way. A helicopter with marksmen. It's going to be okay. No worries.'

No worries? Ten out of ten for optimism. Zero for believability.

'How long?' I yelled back. The men all cringed again.

'Less than an hour. Hang in there. And be quiet!'

It was time to put my deal with Al into action.

'Will there be media with them?' I bellowed. 'You know, another helicopter with the press?'

They flinched yet again. Dad, in particular, appeared to take each word like a bullet in the chest. Ted put his head in his hands. If I got out of this alive, there was a good chance he'd personally throttle me. Probably with no worries at all.

There was a pause. Eventually, he replied. But only, I suspect, because he thought I was such a publicity-hungry dill that if he didn't I'd keep on shouting.

'No idea. I guess so. Now, SHUT UP!'

I did.

My plan was far from perfect but it was the best I could manage. I explained to Dyl and then, through Blacky, told Al what I wanted him to do and the reasoning behind it. He wasn't very impressed, but no one could think of anything better.

We settled down to wait, which was not Dyl's strong suit.

He fidgeted. He picked his nose and carefully examined what he'd mined. He whistled. Tunelessly. After a while he suddenly blurted, 'I spy with my little eye something beginning with "c".'

'Er, let me think, Dylan. Could it be "crocodile"?'

'Yeah! Your turn.'

'That's okay. You go again.'

125

'All right. I spy with my little eye something beginning with "a".'

'Annihilation?'

'No.'

'Amputation?'

'No.'

'I give up.'

'Another crocodile!'

It was just at that moment, when I was seriously considering killing Dyl all by myself, that I heard the whump, whump, whump of approaching helicopter blades. The cavalry had arrived. Time for action.

There were three helicopters. Two had guys in uniforms hanging out the sides. Even though I had to squint against the sun I could see they were armed to the teeth.

The third helicopter kept back from the other two. It had a logo of some kind splashed over the side, and I thought I spied a television camera poking from the open doorway. I got to my feet. Now the time had come I didn't relish this, but those guys would probably open fire soon. The longer I waited, the greater the chance someone would get hurt.

'Now you know what you're doing, Dyl?' I said. 'As soon as I start, you leg it towards Dad, okay? You'll be safe as soon as you get some distance away. Al has promised you'll come to no harm.'

'Sure, Marc,' said Dylan.

'And Blacky? You just slip off. Disguise yourself as a palm tree, or something. Catch up with me later.'

'Fine, tosh.'

'Are you certain Al will keep his end of the bargain?'

Blacky scratched leisurely behind one ear.

'Well, as certain as I can be. Given that he's a killing machine with a mind that doesn't work in ways we could possibly understand.'

'You couldn't have just lied, could you, Blacky? You know, "Absolutely guaranteed, Marc. No chance of anything going wrong."'

'Hey, tosh. I'm not human. Lying doesn't come as easily to me as it does to you.'

'Well, here goes. Wish me luck.'

'You're going to need it, mush,' said Blacky.

And, on that cheery note, I threw myself onto Al's back.

I am probably one of the few people in the world who can talk about this from first-hand experience, but a croc's back is sharp and lumpy. All those ridges down its spine. At least it gave me something to hang on to as Al slipped under the water. As you may understand, I wasn't in a position to see what went on around me. Only later did Blacky tell me that the other crocs disappeared into the murky water within seconds. Blacky himself melted into the landscape. In the blink of an eye, before the marksmen could react, the muddy mound, previously packed with life, was deserted.

Of course, according to my plan, Dyl would have been hightailing it back to safety as me and Al sank under the water. But if there is one thing that's predictable about Dyl it's his unpredictability. I hadn't even got a firm grip on Al's scaly back when Dyl threw himself on both of us.

'Dyl, ya idiot! What are you doing?'

Actually, I didn't say that. My mouth was under half a metre of muddy water, remember. But I thought it. Very loudly.

Al rolled and thrashed in the water. I remembered then something Brendan had told us on the croc cruise. How a saltwater crocodile, when it had live food in its mouth, would go into a death roll to drown its prey before eating at its leisure. It wasn't a thought I welcomed just then. I expected at any moment to feel Al's jaws crush the life from me.

But it didn't happen. I felt my hand slip from Al's back. I caught the briefest glimpse of him powering through the water. It was difficult to believe that something so clumsy on land could be so delicate and graceful. But I didn't think this long. Dyl and I spluttered to the surface. We stood up to our shoulders in muddy water. I flung my wet hair from my face with a shake of my head. I looked around, but no movement disturbed our surroundings. We were alone.

And then I saw Dad splashing towards me. I wanted to tell him to go back, that the deal with Al had involved me, not him, and that death could rear up before him at any moment.

But it wouldn't have done any good. Dad was coming and he'd have fought through a battalion of crocs to get to me. Luckily, he didn't have to.

Maybe Al really *did* believe in respect for the family.

The next six days were a blur. Even now, I have trouble sorting out what happened and when.

Dad hugged me so hard I thought he'd break my ribs. He couldn't speak. Then we trudged about half a kilometre to where Ted had parked the four-wheel drive and drove back to the resort. Mum immediately had a go at finishing off what Dad couldn't quite manage. It seemed they would succeed where a bunch of crocs had failed – crushing the life out of me and Dyl. Then, just when I managed to catch my breath, Rose and Cy Ob Han took their turn, Cy trembling throughout. I found out later that as soon as she was away from the crocs she had come out of her paralysis. Apparently, she'd screamed for an hour.

'You're a hero, Marcus,' she said again and again, crushing my head into her boobs.

'The Force, with me it was,' I managed to croak. Yuck. Being hugged by my sister and her friend was worse than getting up close and personal with a man-eating saltie. You'd think me and Dyl had suffered enough.

Murray just shook me by the hand. Our eyes met, he gave a small nod and ran a hand over his head. Then he walked away.

Everyone else in the resort wanted a piece of the action. They were forming queues just to hug us. Luckily, the authorities whisked us out of there quick smart. They took us in a helicopter to Darwin Hospital to get checked over. Apparently, crocs' teeth carry all sorts of stuff that can cause infections. I should have recommended flossing to Al when I had the chance. We didn't have a scratch on us, but no one wanted to take that risk. The rest of my family followed in another helicopter. I worried Dyl would get another severe bout of his flying phobia but he isn't that predictable. Instead, he wanted to hang out of the door the way the marksmen had done. The pilot wouldn't let him.

'No fun,' Dyl moaned.

I started to get some idea of the publicity we'd caused when an ambulance took us the final couple of kilometres to the hospital. There were reporters and camera crews everywhere. Just getting out of the helicopter and into the ambulance was like being caught in a severe electrical storm – the flashes from cameras nearly blinded us and reporters were yelling stuff like, 'How do you feel about being a hero, Marcus?' This struck me as the dumbest question you could possibly imagine. Was that the best they could do? Still, as me and Dyl were hustled through the crowds, I managed to shout, 'We must protect the saltwater crocodile!'

I thought that would be enough to arouse the media's curiosity. Boy, I wasn't wrong.

The hospital gave us a good going-over, but they only found out what me and Dyl already knew. We were fine. Even so, we were in there a few hours. Finally, a couple of taxis took us to a hotel in the city. I have no idea who arranged this or paid for it. Reporters were yelling, flashbulbs going off as we were bustled inside. As soon as we got into the rooms – three with harbour views – the phones rang. Dad picked up.

'No comment,' he said after a while. 'Please respect our privacy.'

As soon as he put the phone down, it rang again. Eventually he had to instruct the hotel not to put any calls through. Even then, I didn't *really* understand what I had set in motion. It was only when we turned on the television that I began to fully appreciate the media frenzy.

Me and Dyl were headline news. They showed footage of us apparently wrestling a huge crocodile, disappearing beneath the surface of the water and then bobbing up like jack-in-the-boxes. They showed us getting out of the helicopter and I was particularly pleased when there was a big close-up of me yelling how we need to protect the saltie. Later on, of course, I understood this was the tip of the iceberg. That film was shown all over Australia. It was shown in England and America and France and South Africa. There were probably Inuits sitting around sets in igloos who caught the coverage.

For a time I was one of the most famous people on the planet.

And then there were the television interviews me and Dyl gave. And You-Tube and magazine articles. The offers

of money to endorse products. Dylan became known as CrocoDyl. They couldn't think of something similar for me and I was grateful. And each time I was interviewed I pushed the same message.

'So, Marcus, how does it feel to be a hero around the world?'

'That's not important. What is important is what we are doing to the natural world, the damage we are inflicting. It has to stop.'

'It's great that you are an eco-warrior. Do you think this will help you get girlfriends?'

'Listen. The saltwater crocodile is a magnificent creature. Yet the government is seriously considering allowing wealthy people to shoot them for trophies. Big-game hunters who aren't killing for food, but for the fun of it. The fun of it! We think we are the most highly developed animal on the planet, but no other animal kills for pleasure. They kill to eat. They kill to survive. How can we seriously believe we are civilised if we allow this to go on?'

'But, Marcus, the saltwater crocodile is not an endangered animal. It's not as if we are hunting them to extinction.'

'People are not endangered animals either. Maybe we should allow wealthy big-game hunters to kill people as well. It would be good sport and who'd miss a few people?'

'That's a remarkable attitude for someone who was nearly killed by a crocodile. I believe you insisted that the crocs who attacked you should not be hunted down.'

'That's right. They did nothing wrong. I was in their territory. What should I expect from a wild animal when I'm in his habitat? If I go to the zoo, I don't hop into the lion enclosure

to enjoy a close-up. And, frankly, if I did then I'd only have myself to blame if it all went belly-up. Or belly-ripped-up.'

'So you don't think even rogue crocs who kill people should be culled?'

'Tell you what. You find a saltwater croc in your front room watching TV or raiding your fridge for a bite to eat, then shoot him. But if they respect our space, maybe we should respect theirs.'

'And CrocoDyl. What are your views?'

'I'd never seen a crocodile in the wild before. I would like to think my children and my children's children might be similarly blessed.'

My mouth hung open when he said that. But I guess I shouldn't have been surprised. Having Dyl as a best mate should have made me immune to suprises.

Dyl took to the media like a croc to water.

He was brilliant.

He was persuasive.

He was amazing.

The support we received was amazing as well. Pretty soon there were questions being asked in Parliament. Pretty soon the Government announced that plans to allow selective killing of saltwater crocodiles had been shelved. One minister even said, 'How can we believe we are civilised if we allow this? It has taken a couple of children to make us understand an important truth.'

How cool was that?

When I'd sat on that mudbank, surrounded by crocodiles and one very smelly dog, I'd thought about Al's words. The

135

communication revolution. And how I could use it to give Al what he wanted. It wasn't an unreasonable request. Don't kill us just because you can. But who would listen? People had tried to get this message over before, but it wasn't news. So I realised I had to make it news. And what better story could there be than a small boy – two small boys, as it turned out – wrestling a croc and living to tell the tale?

I thought it would create publicity.

I never thought it would bring about dramatic change in such a short time.

It was a relief to return to something like normality.

Christmas at the Branaghan Wilderness Resort.

Yes, we had gone back to finish the holiday. To be honest, no one felt like going home. For one thing, we were sick of being under a media spotlight and the resort was out woop-woop. It was quiet there. It was peaceful. We were cut off and it suited us.

I rarely followed the news, particularly after the fuss slowed down. But I did catch a story in the local newspaper. It was only one small column, tucked away on page seven. A man, a doctor apparently, had announced the establishment of a charitable trust that he was personally funding. The charity would provide sick children and their families with the opportunity to see endangered animals in their natural habitats. 'I have given up travelling myself,' said the doctor. 'But I would like others to experience some of our natural wonders, before it is too late.'

I smiled. Murray had remembered my Christmas present.

I was confident that I would eventually be able to delete

those photographs on my camera. After all, he had been prepared to die for us. And I believed his hunting days were over. Did I really *need* to turn those photographs over to the police? *There's good and bad in all of us*, I thought. I had no intention of ruining what was good.

Dyl's parents, Joe and Mo, gave their blessing to us staying on at the resort. They'd been interviewed a number of times on radio and television and really enjoyed themselves. When Dad asked over the phone if they were mad about their son being nearly eaten by a crocodile, not once but twice, they shrugged it off.

'Worse things happen at sea,' said Mo, though she didn't offer any evidence.

'Could have happened to anyone,' said Joe.

He was wrong, of course. It could only have happened to Dylan.

Cy Ob Han's parents weren't quite as casual, but Cy pleaded with them over the phone and they finally gave in. Maybe old Cy used her Dark Side powers.

Mum was worried sick about going back to the resort. As far as she was concerned, saltwater crocodiles had proved to be as common as flies. Shoo one away and another takes a nosedive into your drink. All the time we were in the Territory she made Dad check under beds just in case one was napping among the dust bunnies. It was all I could do to persuade her not to check the dunny each time I sat on it, in case a saltie hurtled round the U-bend and took a chunk out of my bum. To this day she gets nervous lowering herself into a bath. Of course, she insisted that none of us left the resort in case a croc was nesting in a tree and dropped on us from a great height. We were happy to oblige. I'd had enough of Nature for a while.

Rose and Cy were firm friends again. The tensions between them had blown away, now they no longer had the hots for Brendan. They cooled off when they discovered he already had a girlfriend – Julie, the chook-dunking chick on the cruise. For some reason Rose and Cy took this as evidence he was a creep and curled their lips whenever he was around. I could only imagine Brendan was relieved not to have them hanging around his neck constantly.

Girls' brains are weird. They don't work the same way as ours.

If you want further proof, Rose's attitude was changing towards me as well. Cy was fine. I'd saved her life *and* I was a media star. She smiled at me all the time, which was slightly creepy. I almost expected her to ask for my autograph. But Rose …

Mum said Rose was jealous. For years, she had been the golden angel child and I'd been a piece of poo. Suddenly, she was in my shadow and she resented it. Whatever. All I know is that, whenever no one was looking, she would suddenly fix me with narrowed eyes and rub a palm over her clenched knuckles. My scalp tingled.

You know what? I preferred that to the possibility of further hugging. It was good to have my sister back. Rose being nice to me? More than slightly creepy.

We opened our Christmas presents on the verandah of Mum and Dad's cabin. After Dad had swept it for lurking salties, naturally.

I got some great stuff. I always get great stuff. But the best part was Dylan's reaction when he opened his pressies. I mean, they weren't really expensive or anything. But he got loads of them. Even Rose and Cy had bought him stuff. They'd got him a cool model of a crocodile on a stand. And the stand had a little plaque on it. CrocoDyl, it said. They must have got it done while we were in Darwin.

I'd wanted to shop in Darwin, but the price of fame was that I had to stay in the hotel. However, I'd given Mum firm instructions. Dyl opened my presents – the boxer shorts, T-shirt and other stuff with cola logos on it. I kept one present back and gave it to him last. He ripped the paper from the small gift and sucked in his breath.

'Cool,' said Dyl. 'This is totally cool, Marc.'

The Swiss Army knife was top of the range. It had dozens of gizmos, though I'd no idea what most of them were for.

'I bet it's got something for taking stones out of horse's hooves,' said Dyl.

'I think,' said Dad, 'it's got a blade for taking boys out of crocodiles' throats.'

'Really?' said Dyl.

'No,' we all said together.

'It's brilliant. Thanks.' Then Dyl's face fell. 'How am I going to get it back home, though?'

I handed him an envelope. It had stamps on it. And Dyl's address.

'Ted says he's happy to stick this in the post when we go. Actually, he said "no worries".'

Then something really strange happened. Dylan produced a clumsily giftwrapped present. He shoved it at me, his face twisted and he ran. He blundered off the verandah, down the path and into our cabin. I was so shocked, I'd got halfway to my feet before Mum's hand pressed me back into my chair.

'I think he's embarrassed,' she whispered into my ear. 'This is the only present he's brought. Give him time, love. Open it and talk to him later.'

I did. It was a book. An obviously second-hand book. It had a sticker with the book exchange logo on it. Inside, some strange hand had written, "For Jim on his fiftieth birthday." The price was still on it. Eight dollars fifty cents. And a promise to give me three dollars back if I exchanged it.

The book was titled *Endangered Animals of Australia*. It had been published in 1992.

It was the best Christmas present I'd ever received.

When I eventually knocked on the door, heard the muffled 'Come in' and opened up, Dyl looked as though he'd been having his own private Christmas party. Cola cans littered the bedside cabinet.

Blacky was curled up on my bed, examining his bum with considerable interest.

I hadn't seen him since the episode with Al. Now it appeared he was still bunking down in our cabin.

'I'm happy to see you, tosh,' he said, extracting his head from his rear end.

'Really?'

'Yes. I couldn't operate the air-conditioning.'

Mongrel!

Still, it was the season of goodwill.

'Merry Christmas, guys,' I said.

'What?' said Blacky. 'Peace and goodwill to all men? How about peace and goodwill to all living things? How about ...'

'Blacky,' I said. 'Shut up, okay? Just shut up. For once in your miserable life.'

So much for goodwill!

'You'd think that on this day, of all days, you'd want to listen to reason, tosh. But once a human, always a human, I guess.'

I held up my hand.

'You want reason?' I said. 'How about this? *You*, bucko, set us up. You put us into serious danger by arranging a trap. You relied on my obviously stupid trust in you. And betrayed it.'

'Yeah, but ...'

'I haven't finished,' I said. 'Not only that, but how did Al *know* about the government's plan to introduce croc hunting, hey? I think we can eliminate the Internet as a source of information. I doubt he reads the local news-paper. We've covered the watching-the-local-news-on-the-plasma-TV angle. Only one explanation adds up. Someone – correction, some thing – *told* him. I wonder who that could have been.'

There was silence for at least a minute.

'The ends justify the means,' said Blacky finally. 'We have righted an injustice. Two injustices.' But his voice didn't sound convinced.

'We could've *died*, Blacky. Don't you care about us at all?'

The silence was even longer this time.

'Yes,' he said. 'I do. But … hey, Marc. You guys did an awesome job. I was proud of you. And I never really believed you'd be in danger. Not really. Probably not. Maybe not.'

I didn't say anything. Dylan gazed at me, but he didn't speak. I think he realised something important was going on between me and Blacky.

'I'm leaving soon,' said Blacky. 'Jobs to do. You know how it is.'

'When?'

'Now. I have to go. But, Marc … if you want, I can leave you alone from now on. You know … you've done enough. More than I would have thought possible. If anything comes up in the future, I could always find someone else. Give you a break.'

I folded my arms.

'There are, what, another four people in Australia with powers like mine? Isn't that it?'

'Something like that.'

'So you could afford to do *without* my help?'

'If necessary. Wouldn't be good, but I'm serious. You've done enough.'

'Wrong, Blacky,' I said. 'It's never enough. You come back again, okay? If we are needed.'

If a dog could smile, Blacky smiled.

'All right, tosh,' he said. 'If you insist. Now I must go.'

'Before you do,' I said, 'I have a present.' I pulled a wrapped package from my bedside cabinet and held it towards him. 'Merry Christmas.'

Blacky's nose twitched.

'How original!' he said, his voice dripping with sarcasm.

'A *bone*. Well, gosh, golly and strike me down with a feather duster. Let's all live the cliché, shall we? How about I roll over, play dead and then go and bury it while everyone talks about how cute I am?'

'Not much chance of that,' I replied. 'And it's great to see your gentle side didn't last long!'

'Sorry, mush,' said Blacky. He sounded sorry, too. 'I have been very ungrateful and insensitive. But, as it turns out, I have a present for you guys, as well.'

'You do? What is it?'

'This.'

I didn't see him leave. One moment he was there, lying on my bed. The next he'd disappeared. But he'd found time to unwrap his present for us.

'Oh my God,' wailed Dylan, sitting bolt upright on his bed. 'That is so foul.'

We kicked open the door and staggered into the clean air of the Northern Territory.

ABOUT THE AUTHOR

BARRY JONSBERG was born in Liverpool, England, and now lives in Darwin, Australia with his wife, children and two dogs – Jai and Zac, neither of whom, thankfully, share Blacky's flatulence problems.

A Croc Called Capone is Barry's second book for younger readers and is a follow-up to *The Dog That Dumped on My Doona*. He has also written several novels for young adults, all of which have been published to great acclaim. *The Whole Business with Kiffo and the Pitbull* was shortlisted for the CBC Book of the Year (Older Readers) in 2005. His second book, *It's Not All About You, Calma!* won the Adelaide Festival Award for Children's Literature and was shortlisted for the CBC Book of the Year (Older Readers) in 2006. *Dreamrider* was shortlisted for the 2007 NSW Premier's Award (Ethel Turner Award). Another novel for older readers, *Ironbark*, was published in June 2008, followed by *Cassie* in November 2008.

Barry once nearly tripped over a five-metre crocodile sunning itself on a riverbank outside Darwin. He didn't hang around to chat. Instead, he ran the twenty kilometres home as his pants needed changing.

DATE DUE

0 3 1 2 2 0		
0 9 1 2 2 0		
		RAECO